What Scares the Boogey Man?

Perseid Press
P.O. Box 584
Centerville MA 02632

WHAT SCARES THE BOOGEYMAN?
Copyright © 2013, John Manning

First Perseid Press trade paperback edition, 2013
First Perseid Press Kindle edition, 2013
First Perseid Press ePub edition, 2013

A Perseid Press Original

ISBN-10: 0988755033
ISBN-13: 978-0-9887550-3-1

Book design by Sarah Hulcy; cover design by Sonja Aghabekian; cover
image © Perseid Press 2013; Cover art: "Nachtmahr" ("The
Nightmare") 1781, Johann Heinrich Fussli (John Fuseli) (1741-1825),
oil on canvas

Published in the United States of America

What Scares the Boogey Man?

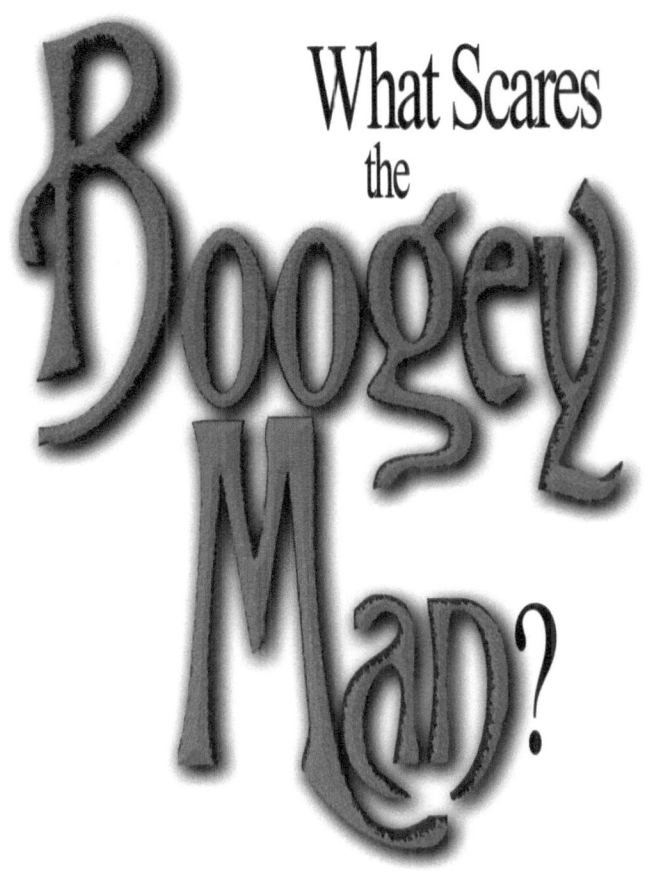

EDITED BY

JOHN MANNING

TABLE OF CONTENTS

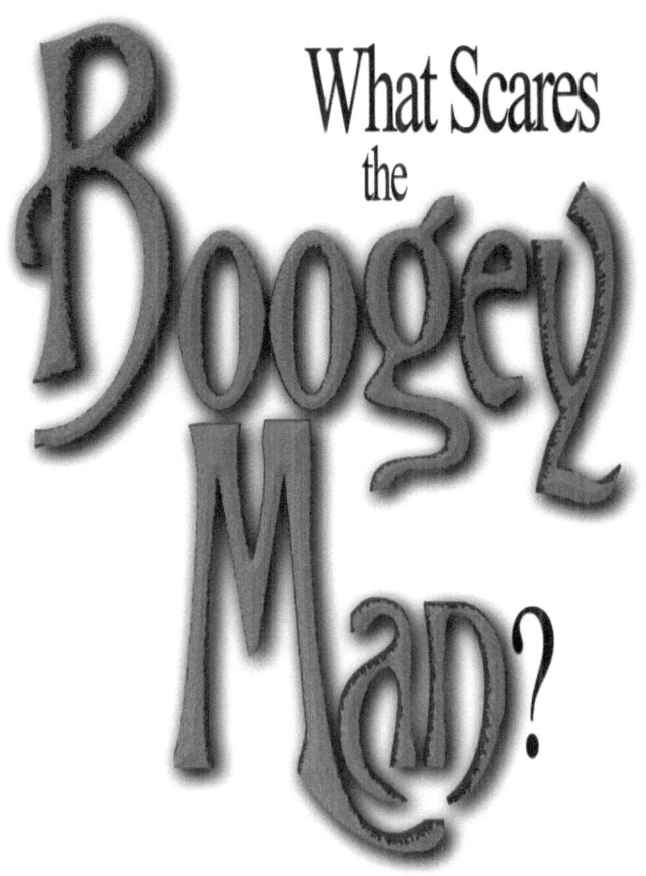

INTRODUCTION

HUBRIS

Hubris is defined as extreme pride or presumption; arrogance. To many people, pride is the mother of all sins. "Pride is pleasure from a man's thinking too highly of himself." This quote from Baruch Spinoza reflects many similar observations in cultures worldwide.

So, what does *hubris* have to do with the boogey man? It was spring of 2011. That January, after decades of struggle and beating my head against the granite walls of publishing houses on both coasts, my first novel, *Black Stump Ridge*, was released. Shortly afterwards I befriended a delightful woman, Janet Morris. I have been an avid fan of hers since I first read her work in Robert Asprin's *Thieves World*® shared world anthology and her own shared universe series, *Heroes in Hell*. When she invited me to participate in her resumption of *Heroes,* I needed less than a nanosecond to accept. She purchased my short story, "Disclaimer," for her next volume, *Lawyers in Hell* which came out that July.

With two successes in such short order, I was indeed filled with pride – and arrogance. There was nothing I could not do. I discovered that Janet and her husband owned a small press publishing house, Paradise Publishing (now Perseid Press). Feeling cocky, I told her that I wanted to put together an anthology, a collection of short horror fiction. My original plan (which, thankfully, I did not tell her) was that I would write a number of short stories and submit them in a single volume a la Stephen King. In all honesty, I expected a lukewarm reception at best. To my surprise, she thought it was a great idea and told me that if I put it together, she would publish it.

I suddenly realized that my mouth had written a pretty big check. Could the talent and knowledge in my bank cover it? The first thing I realized, almost immediately after Janet said yes, was that *I had absolutely no clue what to do next.*

I decided to scrap the idea of my writing all of the stories. While horror and dark fantasy are my favorites to read (and watch), I did not have a stack of unpublished fiction to dust off, re-write, and put together into a decent book. I would have to start from scratch.

I needed a name for the project. I considered a number of titles before choosing *What Scares the Boogey Man?* Next, I had to create guidelines – length, theme of stories, how much I was willing to pay (rarely will talented writers work for free), and the editing standards. The more I did, the more I found there was to do.

First of all, I needed to attract writers. While I was willing to give new talent an opportunity to showcase their work (I was, after all, a relative newcomer myself), I needed some established writers to give the book sales appeal. The first touch of panic caressed my spine. How was I going to attract heavy hitters when I was an upstart with no name recognition of my own?

I pushed down the panic. I knew some writers from my years of working on staff at various fan conventions. A few even wrote horror. One of my best author friends, C. Dean Andersson, a man who has written a number of horror novels over the years, agreed to work with me.

J.D. Fritz, a new fiction writer, is a long-standing friend from the gaming community. She and some friends developed a role-play system called The Lucid Game System which is the core for four separate games. No small feat. I knew that she was trying to become an established fantasy author. I asked her to try her hand at horror. It is her first published story and I think you will like the result.

That wasn't so hard.

While working on the *Lawyers in Hell* project I became a part of a Facebook Group wherein the contributing authors could interact with each other. Hoping to attract one or two of those writers, I posted the project. The response was far better than I'd hoped it would be. Soon Jason Cordova, Michael H. Hanson, Richard Groller, Bill Snider (known affectionately as

Zombie Zack), Janet Morris, Chris Morris, Wayne J. Borean, Shirley Meier, Nancy Asire, Larry Atchley, Jr., Bettina Meister, and Thomas Barczack became part of the team.

Writers know other writers. I received recommendations and contact information for authors who might also be interested. A few declined either because they were already overcommitted to other projects or we could not reach an agreement on terms. From this, however, came two unexpected gems – Robert M. Price and David Conyers – both of whom are authorized by the H.P. Lovecraft estate to continue the dark master's work.

The last person to come aboard, Bev Hale, is someone I've known on and off over the last two decades as someone who attended the many conventions I worked. I'd known her as a fan and as a dealer but never realized that she was a writer. We shared reading time at ConDFW in early 2012. I read an excerpt from my novel and she read the funniest, creepiest short story I had ever heard. When I discovered that it was not yet published and that she was looking for a home for it, I seized the opportunity and you, dear reader, are in for the same treat that I enjoyed that cold, blustery, March afternoon.

Last, and hopefully not least, is my own contribution. I originally planned to use one of three short stories that had lingered in my manuscript file for a number of years. Then something happened. I endured an experience both harrowing and frightening. Once it was over, however, I discovered that I had what I needed for a story for this book.

Eighteen stories, written by authors from the United States, Australia, Canada, and Germany, give this book an international flavor I feel is somewhat unique. A project of this scope is far beyond my wildest expectations. The proofreading and editing tasks were monumental. I cannot in good conscience claim the credit. I have to acknowledge my two Associate Editors without whose patience and expertise this work would still be ongoing.

Meghan Graham, a graduate of the University of North Texas, I knew from my gaming interests and from fan conventions. She was J.D. Fritz's principle proofreader for her game manuals and for some of her fiction work.

She has also shouldered the task of proofreading much of my work. I was very pleased when she agreed to work with me on this project.

Stormy Stogner-Medina has a long history of proofreading and non-fiction writing. A self-proclaimed "Grammar Nazi," Stormy is a bulldog when applying the standards of style. Yet, both women were exceedingly patient with both new writers and foreign language writers. They explained in detail why certain changes needed to be made. Most of them were grateful and the stories are better for Meghan's and Stormy's tutelage.

One thing that I worried about (although it became a non-issue as the project advanced) was being certain that new writers were treated the same as the established pros and all of those in between. Knowing both Meghan and Stormy as I have for many years, I had no doubts that they would do their work without regard to the stature of the writers. I did not want any writers to think a particular work received a more lenient scrutiny simply because the author was already established. To that end I instituted a policy: All submissions came to me, first. I then made a copy from which I removed anything that would identify who submitted it. What Stormy and Meghan received were unidentifiable manuscripts. Even my story went through the same process and received the same treatment. When my assistants were finished, they returned the manuscripts to me. I then did my own editing, adding my comments and making changes if I felt they were needed. The story was then returned to the author for any changes and corrections.

Some writers challenged my assistants' comments. Only three won any arguments, and none of the wins concerned grammar or style. In the end, you, the reader, benefit from their oversight, determination, and talent. I could not have done this without them.

LITTLE ORPHANT ANNIE

By

James Whitcomb Riley (1849 – 1916)

To all the little children: – The happy ones; and sad ones;
The sober and the silent ones; the boisterous and glad ones;
The good ones – Yes, the good ones, too; and all the lovely bad ones.

Little Orphant Annie's come to our house to stay.
An' wash the cups an' saucers up, an' brush the crumbs away,
An' shoo the chickens off the porch, an' dust the hearth, an' sweep,
An' make the fire, an' bake the bread, an' earn her board-an'-keep;
An' all us other childern, when the supper-things is done,
We set around the kitchen fire an' has the mostest fun
A-list'nin' to the witch-tales 'at Annie tells about,
An' the Gobble-uns 'at gits you
Ef you
Don't
Watch
Out!

Wunst they wuz a little boy wouldn't say his prayers,
An' when he went to bed at night, away up-stairs,
His Mammy heerd him holler, an' his Daddy heerd him bawl,
An' when they turn't the kivvers down, he wuzn't there at all!
An' they seeked him in the rafter-room, an' cubby hole, an' press,
An' they seeked him up the chimbly-flue, an' ever' wheres, I guess;
But all they ever found wuz thist his pants an' roundabout:

An' the Gobble-uns 'll git you
Ef you
Don't
Watch
Out!

An' one time a little girl 'ud allus laugh an' grin,
An' make fun of ever' one, an' all her blood an' kin;
An' wunst, when they was "company," an' ole folks wuz there,
She mocked 'em an' shocked 'em, an' said she didn't care!
An' thist as she kicked her heels, an' turn't to run an' hide,
They wuz two great big Black Things a-standin' by her side,
An' they snatched her through the ceilin' 'fore she knowed what she's about!
An' the Gobble-uns 'll git you
Ef you
Don't
Watch
Out!

An' little Orphant Annie says, when the blaze is blue,
An' the lamp-wick sputters, an' the wind goes woo-oo!
An' you hear the crickets quit, an' the moon is gray,
An' the lightnin'-bugs in dew is all squenched away, –
You better mind yer parents, an' yer teachurs fond an' dear,
An' churish them 'at loves you, an' dry the orphant's tear,
An' he'p the pore an' needy ones 'at clusters all about,
Er the Gobble-uns 'll git you
Ef you
Don't
Watch
Out!

My paternal grandmother, Anne Manning, who was born in 1907 in rural Kentucky, used to recite this poem to my sister and me when we were very small. In her version, however, instead of Gobble-uns 'at gits you, it was "The Boogey Man'll get you..."
J.M.

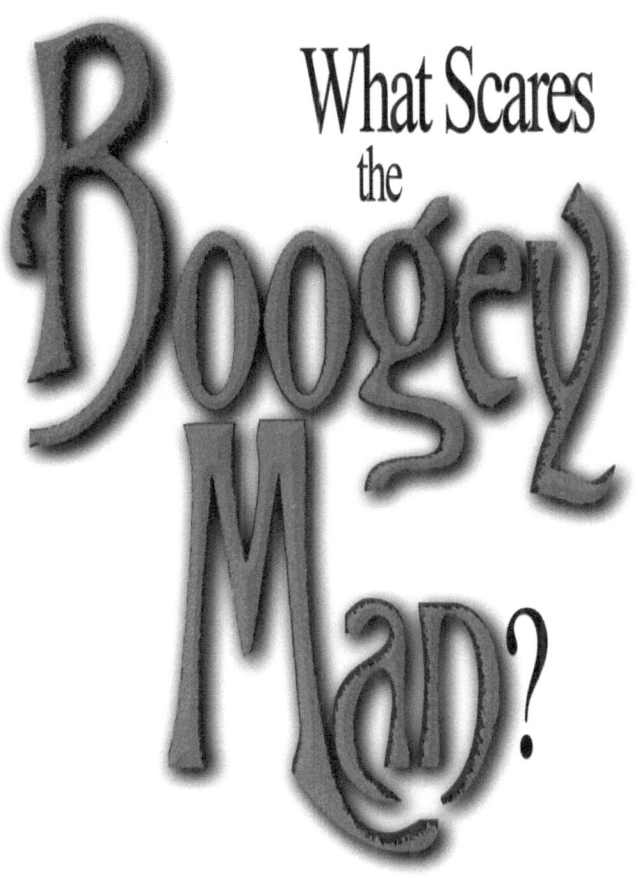

BOOGEY MAN BLUES

by

Janet Morris

> *So farewell hope, and with hope farewell fear,*
> *Farewell remorse, all good to me is lost.*
> *Evil, be thou my good.*
> – John Milton, *Paradise Lost*

"'Tis not easy being me, a Boogey Man, you see. Angry parents summon me, o'er the wide world: 'Snatch up my evil children, stuff them in sacks, and eat them,' parents say. And so I must, till the world turns to dust," I sang, strumming my guitar in an open E-minor tuning as the sun prepared to rise at my back.

A blond boy stopped before me, stared me down, brazen and bold, arms akimbo, while his dark small sister cowered behind his back and peeped at me around his backpack. Their bus stop was beyond the copse. In the distance, other children cried out at play. These two would never see another playground, another classroom: their unknowing parents had damned them to this fate.

I put my guitar down carefully in its open case, among the spit and chewing gum and marbles and coins collected there, and picked up my two sacks lying by. When I touched the sacks, my black claws sprang forth from my fingertips without a sound. I could feel fangs replacing teeth throughout my mouth. "Come closer, you who wouldn't sleep when you should have."

The blond boy said, "Who do you think you are? That Folsom Prison blues guy? All in black and out of tune. I'm not scared of you."

The trap was well and truly sprung. "Come closer and find out who I am. I know you: you're Reggie."

His sister pulled him by the backpack, but close he came.

Blacker than black are my eyes at these times, and the children, once locked in my gaze, walk as if asleep. Up they came, small and plump: five he was, and she a year younger, fair Madeline. Not fair much longer.

"Look in here," I told him, then her, as the sun rose behind, resplendent, splitting the clouds with dawn's glory. The girl held back, as girls will, more cautious than boys, and smart early. Young Reggie bowed his head toward the sack and I had him in my arms in a moment.

The only thing the modern world has done for me is make the silver tape for stopping mouths shut and muffling screams of terror: I slapped a piece across his lips and another around his hands and bagged him. He barely struggled: I am good at my art, and unless they look away from me, they are compelled to my will.

It took only a moment to bag the boy.

She wailed then, did young Madeline, but could not back away or run away. Her feet were rooted to the spot, her eyes held fast by mine. "Come, child, too late for all of that," I sang softly, and she was mine: Little wrists, little mouth, quiet under its sticky tape: now in my second sack, down to her laced-up shoes. These shoes had lights within them and soon all that could be seen of her was the pulsing of these lights within her hopsack.

I slung one sack over each shoulder and hummed away, leaving my guitar case open, to dissolve behind me as it always does.

Into the copse we went and as I walked on, with my quarry struggling now in their sacks, macadam turned to ancient trail.

I'd come this way before. How many times? Unknown and unknowable. Over the wide world.

Theirs were high-pitched, muffledy screams now, no longer quieted by my eyes. Struggling and kicking: kiddies in sacks, my job begun. So I said, as I often do, to these wayward imps who don't obey mother or father and mischief make: "You're sorry now, are you? You'll be good, will you? Sleep when time for sleep has come? Wake when told, and live the days as good youngsters should?

"Too late. Your mummy and daddy called for me, and here I am. You were warned. You heeded not one word. Will they miss you? For a while. You're sprung from loins you disobeyed until the ancient cry went up: 'The Boogey Man will get you if you don't go to sleep right now.'

"And did you sleep then? No, foolish brats who drove your parents to despair. So despair you both. The world is full of strife and needs you not one whit. Your parents called me forth, hungry as my kind always is and always must be, to catch you up and chew you up, bite by precious bite."

A wail no taped mouth could stop arose from the girl in her sack upon my right shoulder. I know what that wail means: "Why me? I'm too young to die. I didn't understand. My mummy and daddy will be scared for me. Put me down! Let me run away and live to sleep another night, play another day!"

"Your parents? You think they'll miss you? They'll grieve, as parents must. You're torn from their flesh. Alas. They called down this ancient curse upon your heads, as parents do around a globe with too many children on it to waste their days and waste their lessons. Soon you'll be part of my flesh, not wasted."

One kicked – the heavier, the boy called Reginald. Slung on my other shoulder, his sister wriggled and moaned.

Now comes my tree, where I hang them. Creatures rustle in the brush, awaiting the scraps of meat to come. Hardly a bone lies here, just a few small shards from kills gone by.

A grisly job, some might say. But we boogey men do it, round and about the whole wide world on every night and day, when morning breaks and fate takes shape.

For eons, I'd listen to the children cry, explain what would happen, tell them why. Not now, I don't.

I took the girl out first: she was the plumper of the two, her black eyes wide above her gag. I put my hand upon her brow. And from that moment on, the struggle went rough with her: she railed and writhed and bucked and kicked as I cut her little hands off and hung her from a high branch by her feet.

It's better when they struggle: upside down, I hang them, so the blood runs out of them evenly as they writhe. Bled out, they are so much tastier.

Beneath her on unforgiving ground is a dark patch where the blood of thousands of children has dyed the earth forever a hellish ruddy black.

And so I do the same with Reggie as I have done with Madeline, and step back.

They swing. They howl. They wriggle, less and less. And the blood pools upon the ground.

Called by the smell of blood in an accustomed place, from the underbrush come the scavengers: a fox, two fat rats, a pair of raccoons. This sacrifice is one the animals revere: a bit of revenge for all those that men do kill upon the earth.

Madeline's shoes pulse with light as she wiggles and squirms, less each moment. Soon, no blood will remain in either one of these children chosen by their parents to pay this hoary price.

Too many children, is it? Across the world entire? Not enough meat, is it? To feed the human race? The two wrongs balance here:

these forsaken children are mine to eat; and I share their butchered flesh with the beasts who hide from mankind and his traps and snares and cruelest torments of all 'lesser' creatures blessed with life.

Spurt. Trickle. Drip. Drip goes the blood of two dying children who were wayward.

Thump. Bump. Beat goes my heart – for in their deaths, my life renews.

When no struggle remains in Reginald and Madeline, when no drops of blood seek the killing ground from doomed children paying their family's price, I cut them down. Madeline's shoes still pulse light. I pull off the pulsing shoes and toss them in the bushes.

Next comes the miserable part of this, my service to eternity: I must butcher them. Butcher them well. Inspect the meat, pink and warm. Choose the tenderloin, and eat it.

Nature pays me her respect, for I do her bidding: All carnivores nearby who smell the blood and hunger gather round me: shining eyes regard me from between the leaves and out of shadows.

A bear stands up so high her head nearly touches the branch where I hung the children upside down to bleed out their lives. Clumsier, her two cubs thrash in the yew, lowing: they smell the sweet enticement of fresh young meat.

Wolves come now, skilled stalkers, whining; with skulking coyotes slinking close behind to share the feast.

So why am I sad when the deed is done? Always am. Always wish that life would stay forever in every body, every heart. Yet this is my work unto eternity, called upon by countless mothers and fathers to take their children from them.

Do men not know what they do? Do women not heed their own words?

If they did, would there be boogey men? The universe gives what hearts desire. So here I am. And thither are others like me, about their grisly work.

The creatures of the forest delight to share this feast with me. To eat of those who eat them, who kill them and skin them, who poison them and slaughter them and starve them and torture them for mankind's appetites.

In the bushes, the shoes of Madeline pulse weakly as the carnivores come up and together we feast.

Until the meal is done. Until the day is done and night has come.

Until another family calls me to their service, somewhere else.

A bear cub, curious about the blinking in the bushes, grabs one of Madeline's shoes in his jaws and throws it high. His sibling tries to grab it and, until their mother growls, a game of catch ensues with Madeline's sneaker, soaked in blood and blinking, as the prize.

Like my innumerable brothers worldwide, I have my pride: a job well done, and animals well fed.

But pride is fleeting, and no Boogey Man is immune to melancholy. At times like these, even boogey men get the blues. So I sing my Boogey Man blues softly, a cappella, in the gloaming. Waiting for that tug upon my heart, that tingle in my gut, that calls me to another night, to another fright upon the feckless young who will not go to sleep; waiting as I must, until some unsuspecting mother or father calls my name.

Now I wait for my claws to turn back to fingertips, so I can play my guitar once more.

THE BOOGEY MAN'S WIFE

by

Nancy Asire

Today had not been the best of days, especially for this particular Boogey Man.

Crouched behind a leafy bush, partially hidden by the gathering dusk, a deeper shadow in the shadows uttered a mournful sigh.

Some Boogey Man! Ha! Boogey Man *failure* was more like it.

Bill the Boogey Man. Yes, Bill was the name he answered to; he couldn't even claim a terrifying name like other Boogey Men he knew... just plain old Bill. He contemplated the night with a jaundiced eye; an even more critical gaze he turned on himself.

What a poor excuse for a Boogey Man he was. He'd been teased unmercifully as long as he could remember, and a Boogey Man's memory is exceptionally long. And teased for what? It wasn't exactly *for* anything... it was all about the *absence* of things.

Bill lifted one hand and stared at his claws. Claws? He could hardly grow claws longer than some human women's carefully cultivated fingernails. No matter how he tried, he couldn't coax his claws to extend any farther. And, to top it all off, he could barely retract them, which made emerging into human society dangerous, save in winter when he could wear gloves. Passing as a human, albeit an ugly one, was a skill he had never perfected.

Boogey Man? He snorted. Some fine example he was. On a good day, he could scare unwary children enough to make them run away. He couldn't even fix them with a stare that would entrap their minds. They just ran. Those that didn't stared at him as if he were some kind of strange, spooky creature lurking at the edge of the woods. Eventually, they also left, but only at a fast walk.

Even if he could capture an unwary child, what could he do with it once he had it? When he was young, he'd tried eating a child but had suffered a violent reaction, causing him to throw up for hours after. A second and third attempt proved just as nauseating. Of all the curses heaped on a Boogey Man, being child-intolerant was probably one of the worst.

Such was his life. All these years later, he was still mocked by other boogey men in the vicinity. Mostly, they ignored him. The only solace he had was his wife, and why she put up with him was anyone's guess. He figured it had to be some kind of maternal urge gone awry.

He peered out from behind his bush. No children. Had he managed to pick the one area of the park that didn't attract children? With his luck, it wouldn't be surprising. An exasperated parent had threatened one child earlier with the chant of "The Boogey Man will get you if you don't watch out." But, the child had not returned to the park, no matter how hard Bill tried to construct a mental net to draw the boy in.

Another failure.

He'd be hungry again tonight for sure. Unable to consume human flesh, he'd been relegated to roots, berries and the occasional vegetable. That, and a stray rabbit or mouse just didn't do the trick. No doubt this was why he could be confused for something left out in the rain far too long. A proper Boogey Man needed meat and blood. Preferably human-child meat and blood.

Since he was in such a self-critical mood, he might as well dredge up his most secret fear. He was part human. He *knew* it. No matter what anyone said, he was certain his mother had coupled with a human and later given birth to him. Personal inventory revealed no claws to speak of; small stature; less-than-horrific form. No one had ever accused him of having mixed blood. Last born of his family, his mother had disappeared not all that many years after his birth. As far as he knew, no one had made an attempt to locate her. This, of course, led him to believe she had been exiled or, even worse, killed because of her transgression– if indeed she had, as he suspected, consorted with a human.

Perhaps this is why he had always been attracted to adult humans. Children hardly moved him, save as prey, but periodically he grew fascinated by a beautiful woman. Maybe being part human drew him to the females he observed.

He was very careful never to admit he found certain human women beautiful. Oh, the trouble he would be in if *that* ever got out. All things being equal, he preferred not to contemplate what might happen if anyone knew about this predilection of his.

Oh, well. He scratched behind an ear and peered out from behind his bush again. No children. Not a one. The warm summer evening should have drawn them out like bugs to a porch light, but he didn't see a single boy or girl.

Another night without a capture. Yet another failure.

And if he *did* manage to seize a child whose parents had employed the Boogey Man threat, what would he do? He certainly couldn't eat it. He doubted he could restrain a susceptible child with the power of his gaze: there were times when he struggled to do that with rabbits. His only recourse would be to hit the child on the head (providing it was smallish) and drag it back home. At least then someone would eat well.

His mood darkened. Nothing scared a Boogey Man: in this he had bred true. The only fear he acknowledged (and then only to himself) was that someone would discover his affinity for human women.

Suddenly, he froze. That voice. He'd heard that voice before. The hair on his back rose. She was coming: the woman he'd seen in the park for days now.

As usual, she wasn't alone. A human male was with her who seemed to be someone she considered a friend, if not more. Bill held his breath as they drew closer to his hiding place. Their conversation verged on the banal: the weather they'd been experiencing, the lovely evening, what they were planning for the weekend.

Bill held still as the decorative stones that bordered the path. He understood weekends. Children were plentiful at those times. Adults also frequented the park in greater numbers, free from their work for two days.

The two humans paused, affording Bill a full view of the couple. She had to be the prettiest woman he'd seen in years. Long black hair gathered at the nape of her neck, a smattering of what he recognized as freckles crossed her cheeks. He drew a quiet, deep breath. She was absolutely stunning.

The male was taller than his companion, and showed all the signs of being active… as did she. Bill's heart did an absurd little double-beat. This woman, out of all those he'd seen, elicited emotions beyond any he had experienced before.

The two humans continued down the path and out of sight. Almost limp from holding still, Bill watched them go. A plan surfaced in his head: he'd come back to this same place tomorrow, and all the days after, to catch sight of her again.

What possible harm could come from his spying? None that he could foresee.

And so, day after day, Bill returned to his spot behind the concealing bush, patiently waiting for the two humans again. Once a light rain fell and, aside from small creatures in the brush, he was alone. No children, no parents, no fabulous woman. The following evening, he patiently watched the path. Would she come? *Could* she come, being as this was the part of the week when she worked? Yes, there she was, accompanied as always by her male friend.

Bill knew nothing would ever come of his infatuation. He certainly couldn't pass himself off as human. She would take one look at him and either be disgusted or pass him off as some weird animal lurking in the brush.

He spent less time at home now, hoping to see her at other times during the day, but she only walked through this section of the park in the evenings. He grew thinner and even more scruffy looking than before. He half-heartedly hunted rabbits and mice, eating them without any kind of pleasure. His wife began to stare at him, no doubt wondering what was causing this new state of discontent.

Eventually, he began to lose interest in staying at home. The bush became his sanctuary; he could watch the woman every evening if weather permitted. A tiny voice in the back of his mind urged caution: his behavior, already odd for a Boogey Man, was growing odder. He needed to return to somewhat of a normal life before it became glaringly obvious something was truly amiss.

This weekend, he sat behind his familiar bush, arms crossed on his knees, waiting for the two humans to take their evening stroll. Other people had passed, some with children in tow, but Bill's fellow boogey men had gone to ground. Too many children had turned up missing lately. From what Bill could gather, listening to the conversations of adults that passed by, the city's authorities were conducting intense searches for an elusive child abductor. Several times, Bill witnessed policemen patrolling the park. It was dangerous now to hunt, to call misbehaving children away from the security of their homes. His fellow boogey men had moved on to other areas around the city where they wouldn't draw as much attention.

Not Bill. He had rabbits and mice, roots and berries to sustain him. He kept to his bush, his existence defined by the appearance of the woman and her male friend. Since he'd never caught a child, he considered his area of the park safe from searching authorities.

This evening, the weather was perfect for long, leisurely walks. A light breeze rustled the leaves of the trees in the woods; twilight had just begun to deepen. And here they came: the beautiful woman and her friend. Bill leaned forward a bit to gain an even better view of her.

"You *idiot!*"

The hissing voice sounded behind him. He jerked around, glanced up and froze.

His wife! She'd managed to track him down, to witness his spying on the human female.

Eyes snapping, she lifted her hand, firmly grasping a knotted club.

"So this is where you've been hiding!" The club descended, catching the side of Bill's head. "And for what?" Again the club fell, this time on his shoulder. "You useless thing!"

Gasping in pain, he rolled aside, ducking another swing of the club. By now, the woman and her friend had halted on the path.

"What the hell's that?" the male asked, voice raised in alarm. "Let's get out of here. Could be a rabid animal in those bushes!"

Avoiding another blow from the club, Bill heard the two humans hurry off down the path.

A hand, equipped with requisite claws, snatched at Bill's back, hauling him deeper into the undergrowth.

"Are you crazy?" his wife growled. "Sitting here all this time mooning over some human woman! You think I haven't noticed? What's *wrong* with you?"

He tried to come up with an answer, but knew anything he said would only make things worse. He ducked his head between his shoulders, anticipating another clout from the club.

His wife glared in the gathering darkness. "Get on your feet! We're going home and you'd better start acting like a husband instead of some brainless fool!"

She was bigger than he was. She had marvelous claws, which were now fully extended. And she possessed a temper he'd witnessed rarely, but a temper he earnestly attempted to avoid.

He scrambled to his feet, her hand still clutching the skin between his shoulders, and eyed the club, but she'd lowered it now. He offered her a glance he hoped overflowed with contrition.

Pushing him in front, she marched him off in the direction of their den.

He swallowed heavily, not wanting to think of what awaited him when they reached home.

Boogey men weren't afraid of anything, with only one exception:

A Boogey Man's wife.

THE ROAD TO AFGHANISTAN

by

David Conyers

The three days it took Harrison to flee the black desert of western Pakistan, he barely slept. When the saw the dusk lights of Rawalpindi he felt relief; street lights meant normalcy and a safe place to rest.

When Peel drove into the city's heart he was forcibly slowed, melded with the busy evening traffic. Despite the late hour, he passed busy bazaars and crowded alleys. Hindu temples and Muslim shrines were clean and complete compared to cheaply constructed apartment blocks and government offices, with their rusting reo jutting from upper unfinished levels. Mounds of stinking garbage piled against chipped walls. Woman's faces on billboards were 'veiled' with black paint while men were left untouched.

Peel reached the Hoodbhoy Orphanage as it was closing. Identified by his National Security Agency employers three days earlier, he had been assured the institution's reputation was sound. Foreign and local journalists' accounts spoke highly of their director, a Muslim who accepted all wards, regardless of their religion, gender or ethnicity.

Peel parked in the courtyard. His aching muscles protested as he clambered from the old Soviet Army truck. As he unlatched the rear door, two dozen red and blinking eyes stared back. It took the first child several minutes to shuffle forward and step into their new home, and into a new life.

"Mr. Peel?"

"Yes, Sir?" he snapped in a moment of disorientation. Embarrassed, he scratched at the dirt caked to his millimeter thick hair. He felt drunk. He wasn't. He was dead tired.

"Thank you for saving these children, Mr. Peel," Rashid Hoodbhoy spoke softly, with a formal and precise command of the English language. He watched, with a gentle smile, his volunteers aid the children as they clambered from the stolen truck. Many had to be carried. All needed water. A few with infected wounds were attended to with bandages and disinfectant.

Hoodbhoy welcomed every child with a handshake and a few words in Urdu or Pushto. He spoke with respect and love. Each child looked a little happier, a little less terrified, after they had met with Hoodbhoy.

Before he fainted, Peel found a bench, sat and waited quietly.

A volunteer who didn't speak any language that Peel could understand offered to clean Peel's wounds. Peel remembered what he must look like, with the bloodied facial bruises, rope burns raw on his wrists, cigarette burns across his skin, and his tattered and torn clothes. He thanked the volunteer and said he would be fine, explained that the children needed attention before he did. The man seemed to understand, and left Peel alone.

When all the children were inside where they would be assigned a place to sleep, Peel rejoined Hoodbhoy.

"They were kidnapped by the Taliban," he explained, certain that he must absolve himself by speaking out loud his actions of the last week. "I don't know how long they were their prisoners, or what tortures they've been subjected to. I don't speak Urdu or Pushto very well. I can't hope for much."

Hoodbhoy smiled with the same warmth and affection given to the orphans. Peel wondered why. He was a foreign spy who lived in a world of deceit and death served daily. It was his people that created orphans.

"I'd look after them all myself," Peel almost choked, "if I knew how."

"It is enough that you brought them to me. Be thankful that you achieved as much."

"But –"

"But don't dwell upon what you might have done to save them, or it will consume you."

Peel rubbed his eyes. One of the girls he had to leave behind, crumpled and bloody, on the roadside. "An orphan died," he confessed. "She couldn't have been more than ten. An unlucky shot from a sniper."

Hoodbhoy patted Peel on the shoulder, "I know, my son, her brother told me. But you must learn to forgive yourself. The brother forgives you. You saved his life, remember."

A lorry sped by outside, rattled the orphanage's windows and the kerosene-lamps, which were the only illumination, before it disappeared into Rawalpindi's humid night. For a moment, Peel feared that the Taliban had tracked him even here.

"I have to leave. I could bring my enemies if I stay."

"Do what you must, my friend."

"Thank you," he almost choked again, "…my friend."

He gave Hoodbhoy most of the U.S. dollars he had scavenged from the Taliban then departed. He drove the old Soviet Army truck five blocks from the orphanage before he abandoned it. His fingerprints would be everywhere inside the cabin, but he had no time to apply tradecraft and clean it. He was too tired to do a proper job anyway and burning was not an option. Rawalpindi was a busy city even at night.

With the remaining money he bought himself a fare on an autorickshaw. The hotel the NSA had directed him to was cheap and inconspicuous, exactly what he required.

The Sikh behind the reception desk barely gave Peel a second glance, as if he encountered Peel's kind every day. He would be a

Pentagon shared asset used by the CIA, NSA and a whole host of other U.S. agencies operating in Pakistan. Peel's kind would be known to him.

"You have a parcel waiting for me."

The tall, thick set man nodded then disappeared.

Several local men loitered in the foyer. All watched Peel with unembarrassed stares. The skin on Peel's neck prickled when he turned his back on them.

Within minutes the Sikh returned and handed the parcel to Peel, an armored briefcase. It was locked, a good sign that it hadn't been compromised.

Taking the stairs three flights up to his darkened room, Peel entered quickly then locked the door behind him. He left the lights off except for the bed lamp, which was already on. Although the double bed was the most inviting sight of the last week, he still checked all the cupboards and the spaces behind doors, then behind the curtains before he closed them.

After peeing then guzzling the entire contents of two bottled waters from the bar fridge, he opened the case using the combination that had been provided to him three days earlier.

He didn't find the pistol he'd asked for. Everything else he had requested was in place: three passports, each under different names and nationalities; matching vaccination papers; ten thousand U.S. dollars in traveler's checks; one hundred thousand rupees; VISA and American Express cards; and detailed maps of northern Pakistan and neighboring eastern Afghanistan.

A pistol's hammer cocked. The weapon's barrel was pressed into the back of Peel's head. Two simple actions told Peel in the worst possible way that he hadn't covered his tracks thoroughly enough.

"Looking for this, Peel?" asked the silhouetted stranger.

Peel raised his hands, "You mean the handgun?"

"Yes. No surprise, then, that I've already been through your briefcase?"

"You left the money?"

"I'm being paid well enough."

Peel identified the accent as Eastern United States, and this troubled him. The assassin had to have connections within the NSA. Perhaps he even worked for them. Otherwise there was no possibility he could have broken into the briefcase without damaging it. Peel would have noticed.

When he turned to examine the stranger, a fist punched him hard in the kidney. Pain needled through his right side and he went down.

"I didn't say you could look at me."

On his knees, Peel was thankful that he had not fallen further. The closer he was to the floor, the hardier it would be to overcome his foe.

"I don't think I need to," Peel winched. "I know who you are. You're Dirk Kinsella."

The shadowy figure lifted Peel by his shirt collar, manhandled him expertly onto the bed's lumpy mattress. He stood back just as quickly, weapon trained on Peel's chest.

"Empty your pockets."

Despite his pain, Peel did so. He had nothing of value except some loose rupees. His satellite telephone, stolen from the Taliban, was his only other possession. It already rested on the bedside table.

"Sit on your hands."

Peel complied.

The assassin found a chair and sat. His 9mm automatic remained leveled at Peel's heart. His face, now visible in the dim light, wore a sardonic grin.

"You guessed right, Mr. Peel, the name is Dirk Kinsella. At least that's one name I'm commonly known by."

"So, you're here to kill me?" Peel asked, not sure if he was ready for the answer to this question. He tried to ignore the swimming feeling in his head, of tiredness and exhaustion, even though he was again in mortal danger and adrenalin should have kept him alert.

"Most certainly. These days not many people get to know me who don't die shortly afterwards."

"A contract?"

He nodded, "Nothing personal, if that is what you mean."

"A killing is always personal to someone. Can you tell me who?"

Finally a laugh, as if Kinsella had been waiting to gloat from the onset, "I'm too much the professional to tell you that kind of information."

Despite the assassin's western clothes, they had a cheap, local cut. His hair was dyed black and his skin tanned. His resemblance to a Pakistani middleclass businessman was near perfect. Peel remembered where he had seen Kinsella before; downstairs in reception not less than fifteen minutes earlier.

"However, Peel, I first have to make a telephone call. This client was very specific. He insisted that when I found you, I had to call him to confirm the termination order."

"Is that so?"

"If he's in a good mood, he might change his mind and you might even live through this night. But I don't think so."

During their exchange Peel had wasted no time assessing the room. Unfortunately there was nothing that he might use as a weapon or a means of escape. Kinsella had been thorough.

"Is that why I'm still alive, because your client is indecisive?"

"Yes… and…" Kinsella hesitated, uncertain for the first time.

"What?"

"And because I wanted to ask you something."

"Ask me something?" said Peel, confused. "You're the one holding the gun. What do you want to know?"

"I want to know what exactly happened to you, on the road to Afghanistan, three days ago."

Peel snorted, "You sure? I don't think you'll believe me if I told you."

"Oh, I think I will."

Peel stared at Kinsella for a very long time, searched for any clues that the man was insincere in his request. He found none.

"So you know what it was in that other truck?"

Kinsella nodded.

"Okay then. I'll tell you. For two days…"

*

Two days without sight left Peel unprepared for the searing desert sunlight. When the back door of the truck was unlatched and the canvas bag was torn from his head, he couldn't see at first, because it was too bright.

Men argued in what sounded to be Urdu. A cool breeze blew on his face. Distances felt vast.

He stilled himself when he heard the unmistakable sound of bullets being chambered into assault rifles. Instinctively he tugged again the thick rope about his wrists, but there was no give.

When his eyes adjusted to the light, he saw he was outside on a desolate road. The horizon was a flat empty landscape broken only by black mountain crags brushed white with snow. He guessed this was either Afghanistan or somewhere near or in Pakistan's Federally Administered Tribal Areas, one of the most dangerous places on the planet for a Western spy to find himself.

He turned toward the arguing men. Three decrepit trucks decorated with faded Soviet Army insignia idled on the road. A dozen Taliban soldiers lingered, passengers of the trucks. They were walking to stretch their legs. Each slung an AK-47 or M16.

Two of the Taliban pushed Peel forward, held him immobile as he was presented before their leader. That man's eyes darkened as he squinted at the sight of Peel.

"Khaled Zakaria," Peel groaned, before he spat blood from his battered mouth. "I should have guessed it was you. So, not a friend of Uncle Sam's then?"

"You wanted me to show you the Taliban's plan, Peel, well I keep my promises," he laughed through rotten teeth. "I'm their plan." His soldiers who understood English well enough laughed with him.

"The U.S. Government doesn't take kindly to being betrayed. You still have time to show me those WMD strongholds, and we can forget that this... *misunderstanding* ever happened."

"You're not even an American, Peel. How does an Australian think he has any influence over the deceits and lies of the infidels from America?"

"My nationality doesn't change who employees me, or why I'm here."

The third truck shook violently, causing Peel to shudder. A squeal that sounded to have been screamed from a thousand mouths followed. The truck rocked, rattled violently, as if a gigantic and invisible hand had just reached down from the sky and shook it.

The Taliban chambered rounds, stepped away from the vehicle. As the wailing lessened, Zakaria smiled, "As you say, a WMD is why we are here. I take it that you still wish to get out of this alive?"

Peel flinched. The soldiers' grip on his limbs tightened in response, threatened to dislocate a socket if he resisted further. Peel expected further torment, a weapon stock in the gut or another punch to the kidney, but the soldiers did not hit him. Earlier, while he had been blindfolded and bound, bored soldiers had burnt him with their cigarettes, savored his shudders and whimpers at unexpected, random inflictions of pain. They had only burnt his arms and chest, never his hands or face. That had to mean something too.

"I'm waiting, Peel."

"Of course I want to live."

"That's the problem with you western infidels. No concept of the nobility of self-sacrifice in the name of God."

Peel forced a laugh, "You want me to be a suicide bomber? You're insane."

Zakaria didn't laugh, and Peel became afraid this was exactly what he wanted.

The wails from the third truck fell silent, so Zakaria thumped the side of the truck hard. Then the wails and the rocking started again. This time the sounds were different, a mixture of roaring, whistling and squelching noises resembling burps and farts.

Zakaria gave a new order in Urdu.

Two soldiers opened the rear of the second truck, the silent truck that no one had paid any attention to until now. From the darkness within stared a dozen or more tiny faces; dirty, confused, innocent and meek. Many children squinted at the sun as Peel had.

"Do you want me to kill one, Peel, so you know how serious I am?"

"No," Peel cast his eyes downward. "I believe you."

"Good. So I can trust you'll do this for me?"

"It seems I have no choice."

"That's the idea."

Just as quickly the door to the second truck was slammed shut, trapping the children within. A few moaned. More whimpered knowing that they were again subjected to the unending darkness that Peel had also endured.

Zakaria's jagged fingers gripped Peel's jaw, pulled their faces together so there would be no misunderstanding, "They are orphans, sons and daughters of infidels. They are nothing better than animals. I can either convert them to our righteous path, or execute them, but in the end that choice is left to you. You understand what I'm saying?"

"U-ha," Peel grunted through his contorted face.

"Good," Zakaria released his grip. "I'll kill them all like goats in a slaughterhouse, if you don't do exactly what I tell you to do."

More orders were given in Urdu. Peel was frog-marched by the two Taliban soldiers back to the third truck. It still rocked and shuddered of its own accord, as if the truck itself was the living organism. Whatever hid behind its reinforced metal doors now sensed Peel and his captors. In an effort to get closer, it battered its gargantuan weight against the containing metal. Thick translucent liquid exploded from tiny cracks in the rear doors.

Peel struggled, fought against the soldiers who held him immobile. He didn't want to see what was inside.

"What is it?" he moaned.

"You'll see soon enough."

Two nervous soldiers sprung the doors.

The doors flung open with such force one Taliban soldier was knocked to the ground, where he lay sprawled and unconscious. No one looked to the fallen man. All eyes were fixed on the maggoty-creature squashed into the truck, bound by a thousand chains as it thrashed and moaned to be free. Across its porridge-like surface, short stubby tentacles whipped like a plate of worms, each tapered with circles of snapping teeth, hungry for something, anything to eat.

"What the hell is it?"

Zakaria grinned, "A suicide bomb."

The Taliban general commandeered a grenade from an underling, pulled the pin and held it high so Peel would not miss its significance. He threw the grenade at the monster. It snatched it easily, its many tentacles fighting for it, before one salivating mouth swallowed it whole.

Peel ducked, for they were too close to the blast radius. He couldn't flee, so he tensed every muscle against the explosion that would rip them into many strips of bruised meat.

No one was running. They were all going to die.

After the seconds passed, Peel realized he was the only one concerned that the grenade should have already detonated.

The Taliban leader cackled, "This 'thing' that you see before you, it's already swallowed a thousand live grenades, and many more rockets, nails, ball-bearings, plastic explosives, ignited cans of petrol, and tons of noxious chemicals."

"Thousands?" the word forced itself from Peel's mouth.

"Of course."

"You mean…?"

"Yes, Peel, it's a bomb, waiting to go off."

The soldiers forced Peel onto his knees, then further until his face pressed against the gravel road so he could see beneath the truck. Several sticks of dynamite were wired to the rear axle, enough explosives to tear the truck, and presumable the thing, asunder.

"When we rupture the monster's skin, all the explosives inside are no longer held in stasis, or that's how the American General explains it."

Peel tried to imagine the ensuing fireball that would mark the creature and his passage from the world. He couldn't.

"We are near the Afghan border, not far from a U.S. military base. With your NSA connections, you can drive this truck into the middle of their lunchtime baseball match."

"And if I don't comply, you kill the children?"

"As you say in America, you catch on –"

Khaled Zakaria had no time to complete his sentence. Half his head shattered in a showery brilliance of crimson wetness. A second passed before Peel heard the gunshot that had taken Zakaria's life. Three further shots and three more Taliban soldiers fell into equal stillness.

Peel wasted not a moment more. He elbowed the soldier whose grip on Peel's right shoulder was not so tight anymore, breaking the man's sternum. To his left the second soldier was raising his M16, but not before Peel looped his bound hands about the assailant's neck, and snapped it.

Meanwhile, four further soldiers had fallen to the unseen sniper's bullets. Peel could only presume that the assassin was either a friendly to him, or, more likely, leaving him until last because he was bound.

The first soldier Peel had sent to the ground was not yet inca-pacitated. That man raised his AK-47, so Peel dropped a knee into his throat, crushing it. Then Peel pulled the .45 revolver he spied in the foe's cummerbund and put three bullets each into the chests of the two remaining standing soldiers.

It was all over within seconds.

Not forgetting the assassin, Peel rolled under the children's truck, using the bloody mound of dead Taliban as cover. When he spied a fallen knife, he cut his bonds, not caring that he bloodied himself in the process.

The satellite phone hanging off Zakaria's belt rang loudly. Peel ignored it. The phone rang again, and again. It continued for several minutes.

Eventually Peel accepted the call. "Yes?" he snapped.

Another bullet buried itself into Zakaria's dead thigh, no less than ten centimeters from Peel's head.

"That's an understanding, Peel," an American spoke to him, "that I can kill you whenever I choose."

"Who are you?" Peel yelled into the mouthpiece.

"You have five minutes to drive those children out of here."

The line went dead.

Peel didn't hesitate when he reached for an assault rifle, but another sniper bullet warned this was a bad idea. He clambered into the driver's compartment of the children's truck, flooded the ignition five times before it started. With the engine running, he turned in a tight circle until he faced toward Pakistan, and sped like a madman to freedom.

The assassin didn't lie. Five minutes was all the time he gave be-fore a volley of new bullets found the explosives under the monster's truck.

An inferno the size of a football field lit the black desert like a miniature sun, and Peel no longer needed to imagine what that kind of death might be like.

*

"That was you," Peel spoke softly to the darkness, when he finished his story, "the sniper?"

Kinsella was as much the professional tonight as he had been that day in the FATA desolation, not once wavering with the gun that pointed between Peel's eyeballs, "It's not hard to work that one out."

"Why did you save my life, when you're going to kill me now?"

For the slightest moment the assassin's eyes cast downward, as if an unwanted emotion had forced itself to the surface of his consciousness. If it had, he smothered it again, held it deep inside where it could not touch him. "Only for the children, Peel, for the orphans whose lives you saved today."

Outside, a tune with Arabic inflections, with rattles and drums, drifted from some distant apartment. Cars sped by. Abusive language was exchanged between night commuters. The scent of diesel found its way inside Peel's nostrils. He felt heightened as if on drugs. He was noticing all external stimuli, because, he realized, these moments might soon be his last.

He looked into the unwavering stare of his foe, "I've been looking for you, Kinsella."

The killer raised an eyebrow, "Is that right?"

"You're a hard man to find. Extremely well-hidden."

The dark eyes wouldn't look from Peel, and yet there was hesitancy behind their coldness. "In my line of work, if you can't disappear completely when you need to, then you don't stay in the game very long."

"You knew what was inside the truck, knew all about that monster torn from an alien dimension. You came after it, didn't you? Not me or the Taliban, just it?"

"Is this twenty questions, Peel?"

Peel took a deep breath, "You haven't killed me yet, so why not?"

"I told you, I have to make a phone call before we get to your death."

Peel shifted his weight upon the bed, an action that caused Kinsella to stiffen, lengthen his gun arm menacingly, "Do that again, and I pop you anyway."

Peel focused on stilling himself, "Kinsella, I bet you know how Khaled Zakaria came to be in possession of that monster. I'm thinking it was a mistake that he got hold of it, right? And it was your job to fix that mistake?"

"You really want to know, Peel?"

He dared a nod, "I wouldn't keep asking if I didn't."

"Well, I guess it is only fair that I tell you, since you told me your tale. It started with a meeting in a slaughterhouse…"

*

The meeting in the slaughterhouse would never be documented on any official record; Kinsella knew that long before he arrived. If anything went wrong, there was no one back at Command HQ to come in and clean up the mess.

He felt that the floor set the mood, a mixture of various animals' blood, some dried and crusty, others still wet. The Pashtun militants they were here to see, although seasoned soldiers aligned with the U.S. Forces against the Taliban and al Qaeda, appeared nervous. They were eyeing off the Army Rangers on the opposite half of the killing floor on Kinsella's side. Everyone present was armed in one fashion or another, with knives, handguns, assault rifles, and a few with rocket launchers.

Kinsella observed from a shadow toward the back where few could see him. Unlike the Rangers, he was dressed in inconspicuous civilian clothes, light pants and shirt beneath a cotton jacket. A high-caliber handgun bulged under his jacket and a fighting knife itched against his skin in its leg sheath.

Four Army Rangers lowered a heavy crate onto the floor between the two parties. Before they could release it, the crate jumped in their grips, as if it contained a frightened, yet powerful, animal.

"Is this the promised weapon, General?" asked the FATA militant leader, Khaled Zakaria.

"Yes," said the Pentagon official, "a new weapon, Mr. Zakaria, for use against our common enemies."

A Ranger corporal took a crowbar to pry apart the nails in the crate. Immediately tiny white tendrils leapt free like a pit of snakes, snapped and snatched at the air with their tiny, circular mouths. The wooden panels removed, a body like a fat slug pulsed and wriggled, immobilized by several loops of thick metal chain.

Zakaria and his men recoiled from the thing.

One cried his faith to Allah.

Several of the Rangers, similar to the militants, betrayed their discomfort by stepping backward.

Kinsella had seen similar alien anomalies before, and so didn't flinch.

"In God's name, what is that?"

"Something rather insignificant in the scheme of things, Mr. Zakaria," the General laughed throatily, "but nonetheless, suitable for our needs."

"You said it was a weapon."

"Yes, you feed it explosives."

"Very humorous. How do you detonate it?"

"I'm serious. The stomach of the creature exists outside the dimensions of space and time, outside of the universe we know and understand, in hyperspace. It could swallow a whole city of explosives, if we had the time and resources to feed it that much."

"This is not what I expected."

The General grinned, "We have a little facility back in the U.S. that contains a hyperspacial wormhole leading to a breeding nest of these things, hundreds and thousands of the little fuckers. At this size they'll give you a nasty bite, take a finger or two perhaps – if you get too close. Otherwise, until they grow, they're harmless."

From the webbing about his military fatigues, the General pulled a grenade and then its pin.

Suddenly there were guns raised everywhere.

Kinsella's hand went to his pistol, ready to shoot FATA militants if they fired first, which they would. Then he noticed the General's Army Rangers. They were obviously uncomfortable, but they did not move, or even appear to want to defuse the situation. They must know something he did not.

"Wait!" the General bellowed. "I can assure you no one will come to harm with my next demonstration." He threw the grenade at the monster. It swallowed it quickly with a greedy, rapturous mouth that grew in size to accommodate the explosive device.

Rounds were chambered. Knives were drawn. Men squealed.

"I told you to wait!" the General shouted, raised a cautioning finger. "As I said, the stomach doesn't exist in this universe." He counted down the seconds with his fingers. "Five... four... three... two... See? The grenade's not going to go off."

Eventually, realizing that no harm had been done, the militants lowered their weapons.

Kinsella reluctantly returned his weapon to its holster. The General had been reckless. Kinsella would never have provoked such a volatile response with a demonstration like that.

"What's its purpose then? Why feed it explosives when its stomach is not even on God's earth?"

"My dear Mr. Zakaria, when you rupture the creature's flesh, that's when all the explosives you've fed it become 'uncontained.' And believe me its stomach is huge, bigger even than the Rawalpindi Cricket Stadium."

It took a moment before Zakaria was grinning too.

"General, I'm impressed. What do you want us to do with it?" He rubbed his sweaty palms together, gritted his teeth tightly. Kinsella couldn't tell if he was anxious or excited, or both.

"This will be simple for you," said the General. "You have know-ledge of where the Taliban and al Qaeda strongholds are in the FATA region." The General licked his lips, "I want you to deliver this WMD maggot, and many more like it to come, to our enemy's strongholds. I want you to decimate every last one of these terrorists, blow all the fuckers off the face of the earth."

Zakaria's grin became a large, crooked smile. "It will be our pleasure, General."

*

Peel felt defeated when Kinsella finished his story. He'd ex-hausted six months in Pakistan attempting to discover how the Taliban were sourcing an outer-world WMD. He hadn't speculated for a moment that his U.S. employers were behind the supply chain, or had begun to imagine there was more than one uncontained weapon in their possession.

"Who is this General?"

Kinsella smiled, "He works for the Pentagon; that's all you need to know."

"Does he have a name?"

Kinsella shook his head, "I'm not going to tell you that."

"He made a mistake."

"Of course. He didn't realize Zakaria was Taliban, with strong links to al Qaeda, or didn't bother to research him deeply enough to uncover the truth."

"Or didn't care?"

Kinsella shrugged as if to say he agreed. "Were you told stories about the Boogey Man, Peel, when you were a child?"

"Of course," Peel frowned, not sure why there had been a sudden change in topics of discussion. "Why is that relevant?"

"My dad used to terrify me with such stories, of the Boogey Man coming to get me in the night if I didn't behave, to keep me in line, I think. My dad was a real bastard."

"You want sympathy? I'm not your man, especially when you plan on murdering me."

"I'm telling you a story, Peel, and since I hold the gun, shut up and listen. I used to wonder what scared the Boogey Man. I wanted to know what that scary thing was, so I could befriend it, and scare away the Boogey Man that scared me."

"You're talking about your father, I take it, scaring him away?"

Kinsella growled, "My point is: the Taliban and al Queda are like the Boogey Man. They scare me. They scare you too, or should do after what you've been subjected to this last week. By demonstrating that the U.S. have WMD maggots, we hoped to scare them, make them think twice about warring with us if they understood how terrifyingly we could retaliate."

"And?"

"They were never scared. They are monsters who only saw a mirror."

"You're the side bringing these creatures into our world. By doing so, you're no better than them."

"I disagree."

"You said Zakaria had more than one. How many WMD maggots are we talking about?"

"You don't want to know."

Feeling the need to stand up and move, Peel shifted his weight, only to have the 9mm pressed against his temple.

"I warned you. Move and I shoot you."

"You're going to shoot me anyway."

"Not necessarily."

Peel licked his lips, tasted the salt of his own sweat that wet his face. "You know I've been trying to find you for weeks, Kinsella."

"You said."

"Ever wonder why?"

"To kill me?" he laughed. Both men appreciated that although Peel was a former soldier, he was not even remotely the same class of killer that Kinsella was, not as young or as agile as the assassin.

"No. I was looking for you because I wanted your help."

Although the rest of Kinsella remained very still, the assassin's eyes blinked three times rapidly. "My help?"

"Yes, your help."

"Why would you need my help? Why would you even think I'd give it?"

Peel forced a smile, "Kinsella, you helped me save those orphans. That means that you care about people other than just yourself. That's a hell of a lot more than I can say about your masters."

The assassin snorted, "You've over-estimated me, Peel."

"I disagree. I work for a secret department within the NSA," he blurted quickly when he detected that Kinsella too had become agitated. "We scour the earth daily, putting down dimensional horrors like the WMD maggot, anywhere that they claw through and into our world hell-bent on destroying it. You know this secret world that I speak of. You live in its shadows every day, like I do."

"So?"

"So, by what you've just told me, you know many of the bigger shadowy players by name. You can confirm a lot of what our department can only guess at. I implore you, terrify us with secrets we haven't even begun to imagine."

"You're not serious?"

"I am. I'm here to recruit you as a member of our team."

The man called Kinsella laughed again. "Don't you get it, Peel? The so-called department you work for only exists as a lip service to the real powers in our government. Players who want to feel that through your group, they're still doing something noble. Don't you know that my boss is the boss of your boss?"

"What?" Peel shuddered.

"The General is with the Pentagon, Peel. I told you that."

"Yes, but I thought he was operating on his own agenda out here, in secret."

"Maybe he is and maybe he isn't. But, either way, whatever he does is sanctioned directly from the National Security Council. The one the President is on."

Peel felt as if ice had just chilled his heart. "Do you know which Boogey Man you're working for? I'd say it's the scariest one of all."

"Peel, as nice as our chat has been, it's time to roll the dice," Kinsella withdrew a cellular phone with his free hand, dialed a number. "Let's see what my client has decided, now that I have you in my sight."

Peel fell silent, waited expectantly until his own satellite phone rang, as he hoped it would. "You want me to get that?" he asked with a hint of smugness.

Kinsella frowned, then nodded, "Don't try anything funny, Peel."

When Peel answered, it was obvious who was on the end of each other's line.

"So, you hired me to come after you?"

Feeling the first moment of relief since their encounter, Peel nodded. "Like I said, finding you proved impossible. Getting you to come to me was the only way I knew we would ever meet."

"But that satellite phone isn't yours.

"No. Since my escape, my boss back at the NSA's Puzzle Palace arranged for my calls to be redirected here."

Kinsella stood, moved silently to the window to check the streets, the whole time his pistol pointed directly at Peel. "It's a dangerous game you're playing, hiring me to come after you. What if I decided to kill you anyway?"

Peel shrugged, "I'd be disappointed, naturally. My offer still stands, though, if you want a job with a bit more soul satisfaction." Peel's stomach churned. It had been a gamble that he had played; his last chance. Perhaps he had overestimated Kinsella's sense of nobility. "Are you going to kill me?"

The killer moved toward the room's only exit, his body soon swallowed by the shadows, "My side pays better. My side has much,

much better funding. Certainly has more clout, and they know a hell of a lot more than you and your people could ever know."

"What about an answer to my second question?" Peel could no longer see Kinsella in the darkness.

"Am I going to kill you?" Kinsella's voice sounded from the next room. "No, I won't. But, not because of the trick you played to find me. And, not because I may or may not have come to respect you and what you stand for, however pointless you're ideologies are. No, I'm only letting you live because of those children you saved. You deserve a life for that."

Peel heard the main door unlatch, lock again, and then nothing.

He could have chased Kinsella, but he was dead tired. Besides, in that last shared moment, he'd felt certain that the two of them would meet again.

Alone at last, Peel looked at his bed. It still looked incredibly inviting. He fell upon it.

Sleep was only moments away.

THE RIVER WITCH

by

J.D. Fritz

"Max, I'm begging you. Don't do this," with one hand clasped over my mouth to keep from sobbing and the other pressing the phone to my ear, I fought not to cry. "I have a kid, for Christ's sake."

I felt one tear, hot and lonely, break free and roll down my cheek in the long pause before the voice on the other end let out a regretful sigh and steeled itself to say, "I'm sorry, Becka. But, you should have thought of that before you just didn't show up to work for three days. You wouldn't even answer your phone, girl. What am I supposed to do?"

"My kid was *sick*," my voice cracked and I stole a moment to gather my composure – not that it did much good. "I had to take her to the *hospital*. I'm still sitting in the waiting room."

Another long pause, and the voice on the other end grew resigned when it said, "Policy clearly states that a single no-call, no-show is a terminable offense. I gave you three. I'm sorry, but my hands are tied. I can't protect you anymore."

"Policy?" The rock left in my belly by three days of sleepless worry and financial dread caught fire. "Policy?! Fuck, Max! You're a shift manager at a fucking Hooligan's; not the CEO of a 500. Bend the damn policy! All you have to do is *not* fire me. Find a little god-damned compassion in your cold little pig heart, man!"

The only reply that outburst earned me was a click from across the line followed by silence.

I screamed something – I don't really remember what, but it was probably something I wouldn't have wanted my daughter to hear – and threw my phone with enough force that it burst into a thousand tiny pieces against a sterile, white wall.

Only then did I remember that I was not alone.

Across the room, an old man with a cane glowered at me; a few seats from him, a young mother with more than a touch of fear in her eyes clutched a baby against her chest, as if to protect the infant from flying debris. A family in the corner all stared, and one of them, a tall man with a linebacker's shoulders, had stood, obviously intending to act if need be.

But most frightening of all was a short woman, skinny as popsicle sticks held together with brads and dressed in pastel pink scrubs, who stormed toward me, her blue and white sneakers squeaking on the waxed tile.

*

Never in my life have I driven that fast.

Anger and resentment and fear put more lead into my foot than I really have any desire to admit, and by the time the first bolt of lightning split the evening sky I had already constructed a laundry list of the people responsible for everything wrong in my life.

Chief among them was Max. Honestly, what kind of heartless bastard throws a single mother under the bus while her baby is still in the hospital? Christ.

When a crash of thunder and a gust of wind shook the dark, it came like a cannon, bucking my little sedan. I'm pretty sure my heart actually started to climb hand over fist out of my throat and I nearly jerked the beat up jalopy clear off the road out of simple fright before I managed to swallow the fist-sized lump back down and get control over my car.

After that, the sky – the world – fell quiet.

Not even the wind dared to moan, and the only sound came from my tires on the road.

In the dark like that, with only one half-burnt-out headlamp and a crackling noise of a busted radio to keep the night at bay, I felt my anger begin to ebb. Hot outrage slowly fell away, receding into icy fear that left me gripping the wheel so hard that my knuckles began to ache and, instinctively, I let up on the gas.

There's just something about that sensation of cold, creeping dread that makes a person move more cautiously, I suppose. Everyone reacts a little differently to the fight-or-flight emotions like rage, terror, or even embarrassment. But, in the moments when we know something bad is coming and God only knows what it is, virtually everyone slows down; braces for impact.

Good thing, too, because, that was when the sky opened up.

The first, fat drop of rain smacked against my windshield with enough force that I thought it was a small frog – and the green, sludgy smear it left behind did little to convince me otherwise. Within moments, that one drop had transformed into a full-fledged torrent, crashing against my poor car like a thousand tiny hammers, each smearing a brownish, greasy slime over the sedan and leaving a stench like stagnant water so thick in the air that it made me gag.

A small, probably more rational, part of me wanted only to hit the brakes and wait out the storm on the shoulder of the road. With the rain coming down so thick I could hardly see the road, let alone anyone else who might be stupid enough to be on it in this weather, stopping would have been the sensible thing to do. But, as it so often seems to do, fear overturned my better judgment.

Casting common sense to the wind, I stomped on the gas as though my life depended on it – which, in a manner of speaking, I suppose it did. I just didn't realize it at the time. If I had, I probably wouldn't have done it.

My speedometer had just touched sixty, when it happened. I caught a glimpse of the shadow through the rain before it happened. Bigger than a man, with squat hindquarters and an enormous head with no neck to speak of, it lumbered with neither fear nor hesitation into my path.

I don't think I even had time to scream before the front bumper of my car slammed into the side of the creature while the rest of my poor, battered vehicle crumpled like I'd struck a brick wall.

The worst part?

I don't remember what happened next. I don't remember any pain – although I'm sure there was no shortage of it, considering how fast I was going. I don't even remember the car actually slowing down in the impact, or how I crawled out of the wreckage, or what direction I went after I did.

My next recollection is of something cold and slimy and endlessly insistent nudging me slowly awake to the sound of a frustrated, wheezing snort. The thick, sticky, foul smelling rain had slowed to a constant drizzle that pattered against my face. Wet leaves, slimed with gritty muck, slithered in the mud beneath me as I tried to move. Only when hot breath, rank with the stink of dead meat, blew over me did my eyes snap open. Through my concussed haze I found myself staring into a gaping, grunting maw; hung loose and wide and oozing with a porridge of spit and blood and chips of broken teeth that spattered a hot mist over my face as the monster coughed out another breath.

For one long, terrible moment all I could do was stare.

The beast narrowed its beady, black eyes at me, shifted its weight from one furry haunch to the other. Its jaw swayed loose and unhinged. Each time it moved, it made a wet, grim little crackling sound.

I screamed.

I screamed so loud and hard – a sound fueled and driven by such gut-wrenching terror – that something in my throat gave way with a painful, ripping twinge. I scrambled backward through the mud and muck, fighting the slimy ground for something that might pass as footing so that I could rise – so that I could run. But before my feet could find purchase, I felt my hand splash into lukewarm water, filled with a mass of something thin and stringy that immediately entangled itself around my fingers.

With all my panicked strength, I managed to pull my hand free, tearing a fistful of the stuff in the process with a sucking sound, like pulling weeds from the mud by the roots. Splashing through the thick, almost sticky water, I managed to regain my feet and turned to run. What I saw next locked me in place with a spike of cold fear.

The rain had transformed the oak-and-pine woods that surround the town into a filthy, soupy river far too wide to cross and choked with the detritus washed from the forest. A tractor tire floated past, one slender leg and cloven hoof of a fawn jutting up from beneath. A plastic doll, its nakedness dark-stained and spattered like a gory victim of a horrible murder, bobbed past. A trickle of dead mice, skunks, other forest vermin drifted by, a seemingly unending rafting party of the macabre. An old boot caught against a bent road sign that I could almost read.

Cactus? Caucus? Cockus? Half submerged and faded by age and ill repair, it was impossible to tell exactly what it said in the instant I dared to steal before spinning back around to face the monster I expected to be only inches away.

Instead, the beast lay where it had fallen, far enough away now that I could see it for what it really was – not a lumbering juggernaut from the depths of my nightmares, but an enormous, feral boar, its grey-brown fur matted against its thick body with foul rain and blood, mud and engine oil. The creature's right side lay torn open wide enough that I could clearly see broken ribs and the desperate flutter of meat inside as it fought to draw a ragged breath. Its mangled haunches quivered ineffectively as it struggled to rise.

I stared, conflicted between pity and horror. Its ruined hind body made a wicked crunching sound as it dragged itself slowly forward with its forelegs in a desperate, determined crawl. It gained little, if any, ground.

The gentle bump of something soft and cold against my leg at the bank of the river pulled my attention away. Instinctively, I glanced down to see what had brushed me.

A woman lay face down in the filthy water, her arms floating limp at her side, the rags of her skirt and coat plastered against her sickly thin body. The tendrils of her long, black hair floated in a tangled halo. Without thinking, I splashed back from the edge of the bank, my heart filling my throat. I turned a slow eye down to my hand as the pieces came together and understanding filled me.

There, twined about my fingers, trailed long strands of thin, black, human hair.

My stomach heaved at the thought, at the memory of the sound, and I spun away, bile hurling up and out from my empty guts. I worked frantically to throw the tangled mass of hair from my skin. Damp from rain and river, the fine tendrils clung to me no matter how hard I flung it about and when I pulled the hairs from one hand they stuck firm to the fingers of the other.

Panic swelled up, raw and hot in my throat. I tried to scream, but the sound caught against my already torn vocal cords; tears welled up in my eyes from the pain. A wet, slapping sound from the swollen creek drew my attention.

I stood in place, not daring to turn around. Spinning to stare at this or gawk at that had not bettered my situation in any way. I chose to do the opposite. I clenched my hands into fists, shut my eyes as tight as I could, and, with everything I had left in me tried to pretend this was just a concussion-induced nightmare.

The sounds did not stop. My mind raced with a growing surge of dread with each one.

Another wet, smacking slap.

Oh, god.

A damp, sucking noise like a boot stuck in mud.

Oh god. Oh god. Oh god...

A rustle of water, damp leaves, and cloth.

No. Nonono.

I do not know what caused me to look. I certainly didn't want to. I wanted nothing more in all the world than *not* to.

Maybe it was the same thing that causes every bleached blonde scream queen in every B-movie ever made to walk into the barn or open the closet door or to take a bath with the radio so close to the edge of the tub that any psychopath with a functioning limb can toss it in with her.

Christ. Yes, it was stupid. And yes, I did it. I turned around.

I saw a corpse dragging itself from the muck I watched as its arms, bent and twisted at unnatural angles, stabbed into the mud and then wrenched themselves free, its shoulders working and struggling to pull the limp and lifeless body up onto the shore. The body made no sound beyond the harsh suck and slap of mud, not even so much as a grunt as it struggled. Its bedraggled hair formed a black, weedy pall around its head.

Freed from the river, finally, the corpse rolled over and collapsed onto the sludgy bank. The wet rags that clung to and defined her feminine shape stuck to her too-thin body. Three patchwork satchels, slung over her shoulders, lay open to the creek bank, spilling muck and water onto the rain-soaked ground. Not once during that ordeal did her body shudder so much as a breath. For a time she lay in the mud, still as death, until the lump of fear in my throat had begun to fade. I found myself wondering if, maybe, I had imagined the whole thing.

A concussion-induced mirage in the pouring, filthy rain?

Maybe all of this – the ruined hog, the dead, disgusting flood even the hideous animated corpse on the ground – were all just that.

It happens. Right?

As if that thought was its cue, the corpse lurched suddenly forward again. It hoisted itself to its feet its movements jerky, unnatural
and strained. Silently, drunkenly, it thrust out one foot, then dragged
the other into place behind it. The bedraggled woman finally pulled
herself upright. Shoulders hunched, arms limp at her sides, she turned
her torso toward me before rolling her face in my direction – her fea-
tures obscured by the filthy locks of her knee-length hair.

I tried to run.

Really, I did.

Before my feet could listen, I realized I wasn't about to go anywhere. Like trying to roll out of bed when you've only had an hour of
sleep – something in the back of your mind just sighs and asks, "Why
bother?"

"A good question," the homeless woman spoke. Her voice
sounded like barbed wire and broken glass as her head inclined to one
side. Mud squished between the bare, ragged flesh of her toes, but she
did not advance. "If you run, there is hope. You may live another day.
But what *is* the point?"

She turned, walking further from the river and approaching the
mutilated boar. "You have no job. No savings."

Her remarks seemed more to the animal than to me as she knelt
beside it. The great beast let slip a plaintive snuffle while she ran a
filthy hand lovingly over its mane with no regard for the gore and
putrescence smeared through its wild, unkempt fur, "And, the fruit of
your womb lies on her deathbed."

"H-how do you know that?" Yes, I stammered. You would have,
too.

With one hand the woman caressed the mutilated creature's
wounded side; the other dipped into one of her satchels. A quiet, wet,
tinkling of scrap and garbage sounded from within. "That is not what I
would concern myself with, were you and I in different places." A few
seconds later she withdrew her hand which now gripped an evil-
looking hunting knife, its dented, notched blade glistening darkly in the
foul rain.

"The more urgent question is which is more important…" she continued in a voice like wet gravel "…a slim hope that things will get better?"

Then, as casually as if she were checking her watch, she buried the knife into the animal's throat so deeply, and with such force, that the whole of the blade disappeared into the suddenly thrashing animal's flesh. She looked up at me, "Or, an end to the pain?"

The boar convulsed wildly, but her deceptively dainty-seeming hand held it firmly in place as it fought against Death's rapid approach. It let out a panicked squeal, a wet, choking rattle, and then the creature grew still. I stared, one hand clapped over my mouth in wide-eyed, dumb-struck horror… right up until the woman tore the knife free from the motionless carcass with such force that a few dribbles of something hot splattered over my face. I let out a shocked squeak before the reality of what now dripped down my face struck me.

My stomach heaved, but with nothing left for it to give up, it accomplished little beyond buckling my knees. I collapsed into the mud, scrambling frantically to wipe the hog's hot blood from my nose, cheek, and lips – all the while further spreading the sticky, black hair across my face.

I don't know when she put the knife away. I didn't hear the rattle of it being dropped back into her satchel. Nor did I hear her approach, but when at last I looked up, the woman loomed over me so near that I could see into the shadows of her face. She looked youn– my age, maybe a little younger. Her eyes were as dark as her hair, with deep, black circles. Gauntness stripped any nobility from her high cheek bones as she stared down at me.

Her voice made my skin crawl, but as that one word crawled up her throat and scratched its way between her pale, chapped and bleeding lips, I watched as the flesh of her neck swelled with the effort, revealing a deep, purple and black bruise in the shape of two large hands.

"Choose."

Something warm streamed down my cheeks, and for an instant I thought it more of the pig's blood. Then I realized I was crying.

"I don't want to die."

I almost didn't hear myself whimper the words. Even from inside my own head, I could barely make out the sound over the dull patter of the putrid rain. "Please, don't kill me. Please…"

I felt a sob well up in my throat as I knelt there in the muck, begging for my life. I felt that pathetic little sound – and I hated myself for it.

The woman tilted her head sharply to one side, "Kill you? Woman, you are already dead."

My heart stopped.

Of course I was still alive. I was breathing. I could see and hear and feel and all those things only living people can do. Of *course* I was still alive.

But, the insistence of my higher mind rang hollow. I could not help but wonder.

What if I wasn't lying dazed and hallucinating in a muddy, rain-filled ditch? What if I was dead? What if I was dead, and all of this was real? What if it was actually happening?

I'm not a religious person. I don't put a lot of stock in the myth of heaven or hell or whatever-you-want-to-call your own vision of life after death. It always seemed kind of, I don't know, childish to me.

But in that instant, staring up at the specter of a strangled woman, I found myself suddenly very, very able to believe.

"The choice is not whether you live or die," she croaked, gesturing at the churning mass of debris and filth, "but whether you will cross the river and allow your suffering to end, or will you turn back?"

With one hand, she pointed over my shoulder, back the way I'd come, "Turn back to the waking world, and with your dying breath make right the wrongs done to you. Make your choice."

"I don't understand," I tried to shout, but it only came out as a frightened bleat.

She narrowed her eyes at me, but the tone of her voice did not change.

"Run back the way you came, and I will give you three chances to strike your vengeance."

She held up three fingers by way of illustrating her point. I could clearly see where the broken joints bent at painful angles.

"You have but to seize them, and together we will see to it that your child lives a long, long life." The woman shrugged, and then added, "Or, cross now, and she will be with you before the sun rises."

"How can you make me an offer like that? Who are you that you could possibly do any of that?" I squinted up at her through the falling rain and she stared flatly back at me until the weight of her gaze turned my own aside.

After an instant, I felt her hand – calloused, scarred, and rough with fresh cuts – brush over my cheek, forcing me to look back at her before she spoke again.

"Choose."

THE FEAR OF THE LORD

by

Robert M. Price

The Secret in Sandstone

I deem it the most pathetic thing in the world when we cannot correlate what our minds tell us must be true with what we would prefer to believe.

Readers are not unlikely to know me as a skeptical (and often political) essayist and literary critic. Most of my books and essay collections deal with great literature and political matters, though a couple have cast down the gauntlet to challenge religion. I held a child's belief in God, heaven, and the Church until university years, whereupon wider reading disabused me of my fairy tales and illusions. Having experienced this enlightenment, a simple matter, or so I judged, I was impatient to see other students, equally sharp, who nonetheless held onto their puerile religious convictions. The more they learned, it seemed the more desperate and (I suspected) disingenuous they became in order to retain their faith, or the desperate pretense of holding it. Their arguments (for we used often to debate the matter) were so contrived that I suspected they were trying to suppress their own doubts and to convince themselves by rationalizing. Eventually I wearied of such sport, and after graduate studies, I set out on the literary career of which I have spoken. It was only a few years ago that I entered the ring again. The upsurge of religious obscurantism, as well as the flood of violence committed in God's name, moved me to begin writing on religion and its bluffing. This seemed to me in fact a moral obligation, for I felt someone had to point out that a philosophy of life based unstably upon an initial piece of self-deceit must sooner or later manifest the unscrupulousness at the heart of its zealotry.

I did not believe that the Christian religion possessed the credentials its defenders affirmed it had: eyewitness testimony in the gospels, pagan attestation of a historical Jesus, and so forth, these supposed data being matters of hot dispute even among Christians themselves. My principle objections were more in the philosophical and ethical vein. The gross arbitrariness of the doctrine of the atoning death of Christ, for instance: how could anyone possibly think it just for an innocent man to take on himself the punishment due a race of wicked offenders? Again, what sense can it make to claim that the world with all its horrors is supervised by a watchful, loving, omnipotent deity? One can defend such a deity only by redefining all these attributes away to nothing, and then what claim is being made? Not to forget the hell of eternal torment. What could account for a prescient deity creating a human race, most of whom he knew would be headed for everlasting torment? But I suppose the Christian tenet most repugnant to me was the outrage of demanding the sacrifice of individual moral autonomy – how degrading of human dignity! If this religion (or pretty much any other) is true, then the world is a tyranny, or worse, a mad house.

Religious believers of the more intellectual type, reminiscent of my debate partners in college, began to reply to my critiques in print and finally to challenge me to platform debates, some of them on public television. I actually debated a few opponents more than once, like a traveling road show, which held no surprises for us on stage but which tickled the curiosity of our large audiences. It was through this futile but enjoyable debating that I made a new friend, one Germaine Caulkins, a deservedly famous geneticist who had been instrumental in unlocking the code of DNA. He was, as it happened, a doctrinaire fundamentalist. One could not but suspect that his Biblicist followers took vicarious pride in his scientific attainments, in that he seemed living proof that one need not sacrifice the intellect to serve Christ. But then he never really ventured to bring his scientific expertise to bear in debate, for how could he? He did not even claim that scientific research had led him to faith. In fact, he had been convinced by certain historical arguments for the resurrection of Jesus Christ which I thought held no water. He was, in my judgment, a Christian in spite of his great mind, not because of it.

But he was a jolly and great-hearted man, and I could not help but like him. It did not even offend me when he promised he would pray for me. I knew he meant well, and I recalled a quip from Bob Harrington, the comedic "Chaplain of Bourbon Street," who used to cover the debate circle some decades ago, facing off against atheist matriarch Madeline Murray O'Hare. Once, he said, a pious old lady who thought him too frivolous told him scoldingly that she would be praying for him, to which he replied, "That's fine, ma'am! I probably need the prayer and you probably need the practice!" My friend Germaine returned a good laugh when I tried the comeback on him. A good fellow. Obviously, we had tacitly agreed to disagree. But this did not stop him from occasionally making tactful observations and reading suggestions that he hoped might lead me to embrace faith.

Accordingly, one day he enthusiastically handed me a journal article claiming that a collector in Jerusalem had purchased from a dealer of antiquities a remarkable ancient ossuary. An ossuary was a bone box. Jews in the early centuries of the Common Era often waited for the bones of their entombed dead to slough off their flesh, and then would gather the bones into a stone container about the size and dimensions of a shoebox. This one, the collector claimed, though now empty of all but dry dust, had once housed the sacred bones of James the Just, the brother of Jesus Christ. Actually what the chiseled inscription said was "James the son of Joseph, brother of Jesus" (the Hebrew equivalent, of course). The scholar argued, on the basis of ancient population estimates and the known occurrence of common names in ancient Judea, that a man whose name was James (Jacob) being both the son of a man named Joseph and the brother of another named Jesus virtually had to be the one famous from the Bible. Naturally, as the article admitted, there were scholarly dissenters, but the reasoning seemed pretty sound. At least to Germaine. I was suspicious.

Why was this not merely intriguing but rather important? If the ossuary had been identified correctly it meant that the long-standing debate over whether Jesus of Nazareth had been a real historical figure or only a mythic hero like Osiris and Hercules was put to rest. The most radical of skeptics would thus have been soundly refuted. As for myself, I did not have a dog in this particular race. It did not much matter to me, as an unbeliever, whether there had really been a Jesus or not. Some wise sayings had been attributed to him, nor would I deny that. But the notion of his possibly having been the Son of God was a non-starter if one believed, as I did, that there is no God to begin with. But Germaine seemed to regard the discovery as a blow struck for his side and fairly gloated over it, as did many scholars of religion, who were, alas, soon to be eating their words, just like those who scant years before had been fooled by the hoax of the so-called Hitler Diaries.

Serious objections to the James identification soon emerged. For one thing, it seemed that "brother of Jesus" had been scrawled by a different hand than that which had carved "son of Joseph." This meant there was no particular reason to believe the former was part of the original inscription at all. For another, the patina, the film of ancient dust and oil covering the sandstone box, stopped at the edge of the incised letters. Obviously, this meant the letters had one and all been carved into an old box in recent days. And then the Israeli Antiquities Authority, in a scene right out of *The Untouchables*, raided the home of the collector who claimed to have purchased the ossuary from a dealer. It turned out he had a miniature factory in the back room where he cranked out fake relics to sell to scholarly suckers. This is why a supposed archaeological find doesn't mean much (or shouldn't) if the owner cannot tell you who found it and where and how it came to its owner. I need not tell you how deflated Germaine was. Nor did I rub it in. After all, the disqualification of this bit of "evidence" proved or disproved nothing. Even if it had been genuinely ancient, I thought, it was equivocal at best.

But not long afterward, a truly amazing, really uncanny, development occurred. This time I did not need Germaine to inform me of it. An archaeologist was exploring a site in Egypt which he believed to be the site described by Philo Judaeus where a monastic community of Jewish ascetics called the Therapeutae had dwelt. He hoped to find concrete evidence that might further illuminate the ancient sect. It had been the object, I now read, of much speculation. Some scholars, such as Christian Lindtner, saw in the name a version of that of South Asian Buddhism, the Theravada, or "Way of the Elders." That implied that Jewish monasticism was actually founded by Buddhist missionaries whom King Asoka had dispatched to Syria and Egypt in the third century BCE. Other scholars believed the Therapeutae to be an Egyptian branch of the Essene sect who inhabited the Jordan valley, among whom most numbered the community of the famous Dead Sea Scrolls. (Of course these two theories, though seldom combined, were by no means incompatible). The fourth-century church historian Eusebius had taken the Therapeutae (long extinct by his time) to be a band of primitive Christians and even suggested Philo had visited Saint Peter in Rome.

The explorer, one must say, hit the jackpot. I forget the rest of his tale, but he did find what he was looking for. While no tantalizing manuscripts came to light, some iconography did suggest Buddhist themes. But the real stunner was, yes, another ossuary ostensibly containing the bones of James the Just! If this one were genuine, or even if it proved to be an ancient fake rather than a modern one, the implications were major, at least if one were interested in these questions. And, given what my debating opponents might seek to make of this find, I had to follow the coverage as best I could. At one stroke, all the

56

The Fear of the Lord

hitherto-competing theories were vindicated and merged: The Therapeutae must indeed have been Theravadins, as well as Essenes, with whom James had sometimes been associated. And if James had been one of these Buddhist-Essene-Therapeuts, could Jesus Christ have been far behind?

As the weeks went by, Carbon 14 dating, paleography, and tests of the telltale patina all checked out. And a closer examination of the inscription revealed a clear reference to "Jesus, King Messiah." There was no doubt this was the final resting place of James, son of Mary and Joseph, brother of Jesus, who had therefore really existed as more than a myth. My friend Germaine was, on one level, quite thrilled, as if a treasured possession, once lost, had been restored to him (and on this I congratulated him). The connection with Buddhism, however, was not much to his liking, offending his orthodox beliefs about Christian origins and his dismissal of all non-Christian faiths as simply false. I had to smile, hoping the unexpected revelation might push him toward a more tolerant stance. Little did I then suspect in what direction the discovery might begin to push me, however incrementally.

The Tale of Inspector LeGrande

A few months later, I chanced to catch a program on what once deserved the name "The History Channel" but which had, like its kindred networks, "Arts & Entertainment" and "Bravo," abandoned its original mission and sunk to the level of cheap sensationalism. I was about to click the button on the remote control, as I often had recently, to escape ludicrous spectacles such as the quack exorcist Bob Larson telling tall tales of the demons he personally had cast out, and which rock-and-roll songs each devil had penned. But this evening, the interviewee was a sober-seeming police detective from New Orleans, famous for his crackdown on organized crime in the Big Easy some years before Hurricane Katrina. I was surprised to see him subjecting himself to participation in such a sideshow, but soon I realized that no more respectable venue would have risked hosting him.

The inspector was recounting a raid on some out-of-the-way crack houses in the bayou country. He and his men were taken by surprise, to put it mildly, when they came upon, deep in the swamp, the low-lifes they had sought, and they were engaging in what looked to be a religious ritual. Religious devotion to anything but drugs was not exactly what one expected from denizens like these. So the police hunkered down in the reeds, which provided more than ample covering, while they watched the event unfold.

LeGrande, of Haitian ancestry himself, recognized some elements of the ritual from Voodoo and Obeah ceremonies he witnessed as a boy. But whereas Voodoo was a syncretic mix of African traditional religion and Catholic slave religion, what he was now observing was decidedly more sinister. He thought he heard chanting invocations of Satan, Mastema, Semjaza, all names for the Christian devil. But these were by no means the harmless posers familiar from American pop Satanism, the make-believe cults of LaVey and his merry pranksters.

When LeGrande saw a sudden eruption of blood amidst the general chaos of leaping and diving naked bodies, he decided he must act. It might be an animal sacrifice, but it might be the blood of a human captive. He could not see which from his present vantage point. He had risen halfway from his crouch when what he beheld froze him where he was.

Above the howling pack of degenerates there towered a form of fiery, golden radiance. It had angelic eagle wings and the head of a goat. It was both beautiful and horrible. And, it could not be some special effects projection. Not here. Not in these circumstances. Not with these idiots.

But, now they had been seen! Though most of the cultists were focused on the rising apparition, some few men must have been posted as watchers. At the sight of LeGrande and his men, they shouted to one another and opened fire with the weapons they already had poised. This broke the spell; the image vanished with a blazing flash which set several of the thickly crowding trees afire. Given the swampy conditions, the fire did not burn out of control and even died down quickly, but it had achieved two results. The ensuing melee provided sufficient confusion for the revelers to escape, no doubt along secret paths known only to them. And the blackened branches and scorched trunks proved it was no hallucination that the inspector and most of his men agreed they had seen.

LeGrande, a man of stolid character, did his duty and reported precisely what he had seen. Not surprisingly, his superiors rejected his report and fired him, along with a couple of his men who dared to come forth and corroborate his wild story.

Apparently, LeGrande had supplied enough entertainment for the jaded audience, and the host summarily dismissed him with an insincere, "thanks for being with us." But I for one had to hear more. At once I got up and retrieved my calendar book to see when I might be able to book a flight to Louisiana. I felt I had to talk to this man. Maybe he was a fanatic or a lunatic, but he certainly hadn't seemed like one. And he had made a far more convincing case for the reality of the supernatural than Germaine Caulkins or his fellow apologists ever had. I was curiously disturbed by what this humble and sober-seeming man had said. I still cannot say why I did not simply dismiss it as if it were one more UFO abduction story from a gap-toothed hillbilly. I suppose my intellectual conscience was reminding me that that would have been unfair of me, that I would have been excluding evidence for that which I disliked to believe. At any rate, the bee was in my bonnet now, and there was but one way to get it out. I had to track down Inspector LeGrande.

The next day I contacted the show's producer through the History Channel website, phoning once I had the number. They usually shielded their guests from contact with pesky viewers, but I managed to convince them to put me in touch with LeGrande, or at least to supply contact information. You see, they recognized my name and my voice from my own several media appearances. I make a point not to exploit my notoriety, since I hate when others do it, but sometimes it comes in handy.

By sunset of the following day I had reached LeGrande and persuaded him to see me. He had plenty of time, given his forced early retirement. I felt I had to see the man in person to properly assess his own belief in his story and the likelihood that he had not unwittingly embellished it, as often happens when someone witnesses an odd event.

Three days later, the inspector, as polite a fellow as ever I had met, picked me up from the airport and drove us in his aging Buick to one of his favorite restaurants. It was nothing fancy, but they didn't mind you lingering for a long conversation.

As I sat across from him and absently munched whatever it was I had ordered, I was struck not only with the man's acuity but with his look of profound weariness and resignation. He did not so much mourn the loss of his job and his chosen work as he seemed utterly at a loss to assimilate his recent experience. I now had no doubt that he was not magnifying his story. If anything, the opposite was true; he several times hedged, suggesting that perhaps this or that detail was not quite as it seemed. But, I could see he simply could not bring himself to dismiss his encounter as an illusion. If he wasn't going to lie to anyone else about it, he sure was not about to start lying to himself.

In fact, there had been *more* to the incident than he had dared to disclose, even on TV. He had feared incarceration as a lunatic. What he had not divulged, as he now told me, was that the looming, luminous figure of Baphomet grabbed up several people, both of the rioting cultists and of his own men, whereupon they blazed like flares in his scaly hands, and then he popped them into his open maw like blackened marshmallows. This fact helped explain his abrupt dismissal from the Police Department, since he could not account for the disappearance of these officers in any believable way.

As I sat there and listened to Inspector LeGrande, I found myself feeling that his crazy story was yet somehow plausible, given the evidence he had provided (the burning and charring in the swamp which I verified for myself the next afternoon) and the testimony of his surviving men which had cost them so much. But I also felt a foreboding sense that, should I dare entertain the possible truth of his story, I should be embarking on a road I did not want to go down, to a destination I very much feared.

I thanked the inspector and commiserated with him on his treatment, and the next evening I returned home, all the while feeling I had been cut loose from any familiar moorings.

The next week I decided to meet with Germaine. I needed to know what he would make of the story. I knew pretty well without asking what my secular colleagues would say. At least Germaine had a wider frame of reference. I called him up and arranged to meet him for dinner the next evening.

"Well, Chris," he said, "I guess you can see the implications here. If there is a devil, and I get the impression you're open to that possibility, then there must be a God, too. Right?" The thought had crossed my mind, but I was not about to give up without a fight.

"Actually, I don't think *you* get the implications, my friend. If there is an archfiend who can counter God's moves, thwart his will, successfully defy him, what kind of God are we talking about? I mean, I guess I could almost see Spinoza's God, or Tillich's, more of an impersonal essence or something. But if there is a goat-hoofed devil – and he's God's opposite number, well, wouldn't even you agree that's raw mythology?"

He was quick with a reply, "I confess I never paid much attention to the Satan business. I figure man's own evil is enough to explain most of what happens in the world. But there *is* the Bible. And there's what LeGrande says he saw! Maybe things are a bit more like we learned them in childhood. Maybe we have made it too abstract. I don't know. But one thing does occur to me. If you try very hard, you could probably come up with some rationalization of this thing, but I'm willing to bet it would be like your friend Hume said: you shouldn't believe any report of a miracle until any rival explanation would itself be more far-fetched than the miracle itself!'"

I had already decided I was not going to try to get out of a tight spot by using the kind of tortured reasoning fundamentalists use when they're trying to avoid admitting a biblical contradiction. I was getting a headache.

The Witness from the Sea

I must admit I tried to put the whole crazy business out of my mind for the next few weeks, but it was not to last. I was up late working on a column about the latest Mideast war when the phone rang. On the other end was a fellow skeptic who insisted I go to the television and turn on the Catholic channel. I knew which one he meant; sometimes, trying to escape Pat Robertson's squinting smiles I would hasten up a few clicks and find myself flinching at Mother Angelica, the head honcho of the network. She always looked like the witch from "Hansel and Gretel," if you ask me. But here was the channel, and some gray-robed monk was blathering on about the mercies of the Mother of God, the Blessed Mother of our Savior.

So what? I thought. But I decided I'd best listen to a little of it, if only to understand the jokes my friend would be making about it next time I saw him.

Suddenly I could see what my pal had thought so funny, at least outrageous. The monk wasn't talking about the same old apparitions of the Blessed Virgin at Fatima and La Salette, but of something from a decade ago that had come to light only recently. A Norwegian sea captain had been about to go down with his ship in a terrible typhoon that had blown up out of nowhere. And *he'd* had a vision, too. Like LeGrande's, it had been a whopper! This time, a nimbus of light had formed (the story went) above the ship, cutting through the gray shroud of the driving rain. It formed an oval, and within it there appeared a three-dimensional image of the Virgin Mary. She said, in a ringing voice loud enough to be heard above the storm, "Peace! Be still!" And the wind and rain stopped almost immediately, like bad editing in a movie.

I figured it was a lot of pious nonsense. Who knew *what* had happened, if anything at all? But then two "details" made my ears perk up. *One*: all the sailors, like most Scandinavians, were Protestants, not likely to have visions, or even tell tales, of the Virgin Mary. *Two*: the captain, a man named Josefson, did not at the time understand what the voice had uttered, though he said he remembered exactly what it sounded like. When he got back to Oslo, he went to inquire of a linguist at the university, who told him the meaning of the words he had heard – *in Aramaic*.

You know what they say, "In for a penny, in for a pound." I started making travel plans again. Online, I was able to dig up a couple of old and skimpy reports, one in a pretty derisive tone, about Captain Josefson's Mariological adventure. I already knew he had been located in Oslo, and these internet clips gave me a couple of new clues. I figured I'd probably be able to nail down a definite address once I got there, perhaps from the local police.

On the long flight over, I knew I wouldn't be able to sleep, so I brought a couple of books Germaine had loaned me, *Mere Christianity* by the venerable C.S. Lewis and *The Everlasting Man* by G.K. Chesterton. I had always inclined toward regarding Lewis as too clever for his own good and Chesterton as a pompous windbag with nothing cogent to say. In light of recent experiences, I thought it might be worth reading them through again, with new eyes. I found only my usual objections to faith coming to mind again and again, almost on every page. How could a fair-minded God condemn you to hell for flunking a theology exam? Not having the "right" beliefs? And how can poor mortals ever decide which of the competing sects *has* the right beliefs? How can reasoning adults be told just to put their own judgment on the shelf and believe what an old book says simply because the old book says it? I kept shaking my head and finally closed the books. Sleep came after all.

In Oslo, I went through customs and checked into my hotel. I didn't bother with the police after all, but visited the American embassy, and they were able to give me what I needed after two or three calls. Nice people. So I hailed a cab and handed the driver the paper slip with Josefson's address hastily penciled on it. It didn't take long till he deposited me on the curb in front of a tidy old cottage that bore the name *Josefson* on its freestanding mailbox. Up the slate walk I went, then knocked.

After a few moments the door opened a crack, and an eye scrutinized me from behind a thick lens. I thought it was a woman's eye.

"Mrs. Josefson?"

I pulled from my pocket one of those cell phones with the translation program. I thought I might as well try this first and go off to find a translator if I had to. I gave her my name and asked briefly if I might talk to her husband. I could understand enough of what she said in answer to know I had come much too late. Her husband, the captain, had died of a stroke some years earlier. Luckily she knew a bit of English, enough to tell me the bad news. I managed to convey that I was very interested in his vision of Mary. She motioned me to wait a moment, then returned with a videocassette. I gathered it was a recording of her late husband telling his story for the umpteenth time; he must have decided to tell it on tape and be done with it, just hand it to future inquirers. I imagined there had been a lot of them. But, why a videocassette rather than just an audiocassette? I thanked her and left her, I hope, in peace. Back in my hotel room I ordered up a VCR and put the cassette in its mouth.

I expected to see an old man sitting in his easy chair rattling off a tall tale, and I thought it would probably be all in Norwegian. Surely I would have to get someone to make me a transcript in English. But, no. Definitely not.

My scalp tingled. My arms went numb. I felt light-headed. One of Josefson's crewmen had brought along a video camera for any one of a number of possible reasons. He had caught the apparition on tape!

Given the conditions, the camera work was pretty choppy, as you'd expect, but remember, the violence of the storm had abated suddenly, and the man was able to hold the camera pretty steady for long enough to catch the image of the giant woman up in the sky.

I suppose it was possible for the tape to have been an elaborate hoax, like that alien autopsy thing. Yet, I cannot easily picture these old, poor, salt-of-the-earth peasants having the skill or taking the trouble. Again, that seemed about as unlikely as the truth of what I had seen on the tape. And I saw it several times. I still have it.

All during the trip home, the flight attendants kept asking me if I was sick. Not exactly sick, no, but I spent the whole flight in a state of near-shock. I felt utterly at sea, as if my sanity were slipping away.

Of course, once I got home I showed the tape to various experts, who all assumed it was, if not a hoax, a cinematic fiction, but none of them could find any trace of artifice. Whoever had shot it, all averred, was an unknown master whose skills none of these professionals could match. That was all I needed to hear.

To my surprise, there was an e-mail waiting for me on my computer, from the New Orleans police. Inspector LeGrande had been burned to death in his apartment, though nothing around the body was so much as singed. You know, like those cases they chalk up to spontaneous human combustion. Come to think of it, I believe I first heard about that on the History Channel, too.

Angel Street

I didn't sleep for a few days, and then I slept for a few more. My head was spinning. My world was tottering. Maybe I should have phoned Germaine, but I didn't. I guess I was afraid he might gloat, but of course he wouldn't. I guess I was too proud to admit I might have been wrong about everything all this time. I still can't stand the idea. But I don't think it's pride. I've always been willing to change my mind if somebody could prove me wrong. I've actually done it a couple of times, though never on anything this big.

I decided I needed a rest, so I took off for the mountains, after canceling a couple of major speaking engagements. I tried to put everything out of mind. Drinking helped, but not for very long. I located a Bible and glanced through the gospels, then the epistle to the Romans. None of it seemed very plausible to me, either the stories or the reasoning. I guess it might have been possible to admit the reality of the supernatural without having to swallow *all* this stuff, but then I thought of how the James ossuary, the visitation of Satan, the apparition of Mary – all of it was very specifically Christian, even Catholic. But, how could it be true? And, worse, what if it was? What would my life mean? What kind of a universe would I be stuck in? But the vise was about to get squeezed tighter.

I was hiking through the hills one evening, again trying to get my mind back in its usual groove, trying to plan out a new essay, maybe a new book – perhaps one on politics. Nothing was coming, and night was rapidly falling. I stopped and built a campfire. I opened a can of beans. I dropped it, whole, into the fire as my fingers went nerveless.

Above me there appeared in a shower of light the form of a winged man. Yes, I might as well say it: an angel. He looked straight at me, and he said in tones that chimed like a bell, "Chris, you have been greatly blessed. It is time for you to stop running, to give your heart to our Father and his Son. Will you do it?" And he held out his hand to me.

Where another might rejoice at such a token of divine favor, I cannot not rise from the slough of despond. Despite the light that nearly blinded me, I am mired in a darkness of soul, for I now know I do have a soul. I can no longer deny that Germaine and his friends are horribly correct. Only they are fools not to see the leaden weight of the thing. There is a capricious Jehovah who crushes the innocent to save the guilty, and who nonetheless shovels his children into hell like coal into a furnace. There is a Trinity which we cannot understand but must try our best to believe in on pain of damnation. We must bow and scrape and kowtow to a tyrant who demands unceasing flattery and blind obedience. We are to bend and twist our better judgment to believe that which we know to be stupid. We live in a cosmic insane asylum with the patients in charge. Under the burden of this knowledge I must try to live out my days.

And, after that, will I be condemned for not doing what I cannot do: accepting a faith which every moral instinct bids me disdain? I cannot lose my soul in a bid to save it.

I shall know soon enough. I have just been diagnosed with inoperable cancer.

THE COLD

by

Jason Cordova

His eyes snapped open.

Nearby, lying on the floor, his dog snored and twitched his hind leg. That was a familiar sound, a comforting noise in the dark. Something else had woken him.

But what?

Many heartbeats passed before he slowly exhaled. He had been dreaming, imagining things again. Just as his doctor said. Just as his stepmother told him.

Bobby turned his head and looked at the clock on his nightstand. He struggled for a moment to see what the digital clock read, his vision still slightly blurry. It was just after midnight, he realized. *That couldn't be right*. He pulled the thick blanket tighter beneath his chin and leaned over the edge of his bed. Chester, the world's greatest dog, lay sleeping, dreaming whatever golden retrievers dreamed when not driving his stepmother crazy. Chasing rabbits, or maybe his stepmother? Bobby could only hope his dog had better dreams than he had.

Bobby had snuck the dog into his room for the night, his fears finally getting the better of him. His parents would be mad in the morning if – no, *when* – they discovered what he had done.

Let them be mad, he thought as he rolled onto his back. *Let them ground me. They can ground me for forever, as long as The Cold doesn't come back.*

He didn't know what else to call it. He'd never seen it. He had heard it and felt it, though. He had heard every single footstep it made as it slowly climbed the stairs night after night. He had felt the overpowering sense of evil which emanated from The Cold as it walked through the house. He could remember each footstep vividly, The Cold growing braver and more daring as it ventured further into the house on each ensuing night.

It had taken a week for it to climb the stairs, slowly working its way to the top. Each night it had grown bolder. Each night Bobby's courage failed him and he would bury himself under his blanket until The Cold disappeared.

It had been another three nights before it had finally made it to the threshold of his door. Last night it had actually entered Bobby's room. The Cold had stopped at the foot of his bed and waited for him to open his eyes, to acknowledge its presence. Bobby had refused. The Cold, after what had seemed like an eternity, eventually left, leaving Bobby alone in his room as the morning sunlight began to peek through the window. He had not cried out in fear, though he had very much wanted to.

He had been too afraid to cry.

He had been afraid of what would happen if The Cold knew he was awake.

Fear was a very powerful motivator for such a young boy.

It had only been after The Cold had entered his room that Bobby no longer cared about being grounded for sneaking his dog into his room. As though on cue, Chester raised his head and looked at Bobby, his expression inquisitive. Bobby smiled and scratched the friendly dog's ear. Chester's tail beat against the floor, a soft and steady *thump-thump-thump* in the dark. Chester licked his hand and Bobby almost giggled. Chester would protect him, no matter what.

Thump.

Bobby froze. Chester growled deep within his throat.

No, Bobby thought. *Oh please no.*

He waited expectantly, dreading the eventual noise. He knew that The Cold would come for him on this night. It had delayed long enough. *Maybe it'll be frightened away by Chester. Maybe it'll*

Thump. Thump.

He jerked his hand away from Chester's head and pulled the blanket back over his head. He felt the familiar panic begin to form in his belly. *It* had returned. *It* was back. He shook and struggled to pull the blanket tighter around his body, flimsy protection against something as dreadful as The Cold. He held his breath as he listened to the tell-tale sounds of The Cold slowly climbing the stairs, each step echoing louder than the last.

Why didn't his dad or stepmom ever hear The Cold as it moved throughout the house? They never seemed to be awakened by the monstrous creature, their sleep undisturbed by its intrusion into their home. Only Bobby seemed aware of it. Bobby, and now Chester. Chester whined suddenly. Bobby wished he could whine as well, but then The Cold would know he was awake and do something horrible to him, something so evil that it was beyond comprehension. Bobby knew this in his gut somehow. He would not survive if The Cold knew he could hear it. It would do something to him.

The seconds dragged by.

It was terrifying.

He waited.

Thump. Thump.

A long pause which stretched throughout eternity.

Had it gone, he wondered.

Thump.

Oh God, he thought as fear flooded his mind.

Thump.

Bobby felt his lungs scream in pain as he continued to hold his breath. He refused to open his eyes. He pulled the blanket tighter around his body, believing as all little children do in the invulnerability of a blanket, while Chester continued to whine piteously beside his bed. Bobby could not tell his dog to be quiet: he was too afraid.

Blood rushed to Bobby's ears as his heartbeat increased its speed, drowning out every other sound with its frantic pace. It did not drown out The Cold, though. It never could. There was no way to ignore The Cold. Each sound that the mysterious and terrible creature made echoed loudly in his ears. Nothing was louder to Bobby than The Cold.

He exhaled shakily and tried to breathe through his mouth, hoping that The Cold would not be able to hear him. Bobby felt the air in his room change as his bedroom door was pushed open. He shivered beneath his blanket but held still otherwise, hoping he had imagined it all. Hoping that the suddenly freezing cold room was not because of the creature, hoping –

Thump.

Hope fled.

Thump.

Hope died.

Thump.

The Cold was in the room.

Bobby was too afraid to move. Chester whined softly. He could not look. He kept his eyes screwed tightly shut as The Cold took another step into his room. Bobby bit his lip and struggled not to scream as another loud footstep echoed in his ears.

Thump.

The Cold sniffed loudly, tasting the scent in the room. Bobby knew it could smell his fear. Like all predators in nature, Bobby knew that The Cold could sense his every emotion, whether he was awake or not.

Chester suddenly growled, a deep warning to The Cold to leave. Bobby was grateful, and yet, terrified. What would The Cold do when it was deprived of its prize?

Suddenly Chester's growl was cut off. No warning, no change of pitch. One second his dog was growling at The Cold, the next he... wasn't. The suddenness of it made Bobby tremble slightly beneath the blanket. The Cold made a soft hissing noise, the first noise it had made since entering his room. Bobby waited for something, anything. A gentle, wet slap echoed throughout the room, then nothing. The bedroom became deathly quiet, the air very, very still. Bobby tried to listen for any sound from the great big dog, his oldest friend and loyal protector. Dead silence. Bobby couldn't even hear his dog breathe.

Why did Chester quit growling? Bobby asked himself.

Bobby nearly screamed until he realized that it was nothing but the sound of something dripping. Something very similar to water, but thicker, heavier, like mud in the rain. He had not brought anything to drink into his room for the night. He was not allowed to, his stepmother upset at his past bed-wetting problems. He struggled to think of what it could be.

What is that noise, he wondered.

Thump.

Drip. Drip.

He heard a snapping and ripping sound. It reminded him of when his father had ripped the leg off of a chicken before cooking it on the grill. He shivered slightly, though he did not know why. He did not understand, refused to understand. His young mind was not prepared to handle whatever the true source of the sound was. He then heard something else; a familiar sound on his carpet, very much like when he dragged his laundry basket to the stairs. The Cold had moved something big and heavy, Bobby realized. *But what?*

Thump.

The edge of his mattress dipped slightly as something pressed down on his bed. The frame creaked slightly, metal protesting against the added weight. Bobby held his breath and cracked an eye slightly open as a dark shadow pushed against the blanket. Bobby's eye opened further and he saw that The Cold was trying to pull the blanket back from his head. Bobby fought a terrified whimper in his throat and won, barely. He remained silent, his hands clutching the blanket tightly above his head. Nothing would cause him to release the blanket. The blanket was protecting him from The Cold. That was the only reason that it had not done anything to him, Bobby somehow knew. He clenched his eyes shut and waited. What would The Cold do to him? What could it do to him?

What did it do to Chester?

He could feel it now, the giant mouth of The Cold inches from his face on the other side of the fabric. He kept his eyes squeezed tightly shut, his only protection now the blanket and his own refusal to look. The breath of The Cold was icy, leaking through the thin blanket in waves as it looked at him. It waited. Bobby held still. The Cold hovered. Bobby's arms began to ache as the weight of the blanket began to wear on him. An itch behind his ear began to drive him crazy. Still, he refused to budge.

He felt the bed move again and Bobby choked back another scream of terror. Another sniff, closer to his ear. Inches away. Icy breath tickled the back of his neck as a thin opening between the bed and the blanket appeared. A slight tug by The Cold moved it a fraction further. Bobby held onto the blanket with inhuman might. He felt his bladder loosen and a single tear trickled down his cheek as he wet the bed once more.

Not again, he thought, terrified and shamed.

A coppery smell filled his nostrils, drowning out everything else. It was warm, warmer than the air around The Cold, and smelled worse than his urine. It smelled like... blood.

It was tangy. It was familiar.

It was horrible.

Bobby clenched his teeth tighter to prevent them from chattering as The Cold moved mysteriously around the room.

He wet the bed. The Cold was somewhere nearby. Bobby knew he was going to die.

He stopped shaking. He was too terrified to shake any more. He was too tired to do anything except wait quietly for his death to arrive.

Slowly, the presence of The Cold began to retreat from his room. Bobby waited, too afraid to check, refusing to lower the blanket, to drop his protection. He did not open his eyes. The urine on his pajamas and sheets was warm but cooling rapidly, the air temperature in the room still colder than normal. The sheets smelled of stale sweat and urine, a familiar stench to him: this was not the first time he had wet the bed.

He still did not move. He kept his eyes shut for as long as he could, pretending to be asleep, hoping that The Cold would not be back. He hoped it would never come back, though he knew this to be in vain. He waited.

He waited some more.

Nothing else happened.

Had The Cold left for good?

"Bobby?" his stepmother called out gently. "Time to wake up. '

No.

"Bobby, you're going to be late for school. Come downstairs and eat your breakfast."

She called to him again, her voice firmer. It was his stepmother. The Cold could not imitate her that well, could it? He slowly lowered the blanket from his head.

He waited another moment.

He finally, reluctantly, opened his eyes.

It was morning.

She stood waiting, tapping her foot in the doorway. Bobby looked down at the floor next to his bed, where Chester had been the night before. There was no sign of his dog, no sign that anything had happened to him. Bobby's eyes snapped back to his stepmother, who smiled wide.

Her lips were very red.

Lipstick. It has to be.

Her eyes were very cold.

I had a very bad dream.

"Bad dreams again?" she asked, her tone one of disapproval. Bobby silently nodded. *Had it just been a bad dream,* he wondered. He looked back down at the floor but it was clean. He could not spot any sign of Chester on the carpet, not a single stray golden hair. He exhaled slowly. The Cold had existed only in his dreams.

Just like the doctors said.

Just like his stepmother insisted.

Red lips. I wonder if she has big teeth too.

"Bobby, did you wet the bed?"

He nodded.

"Big boys don't wet the bed."

He stayed silent.

"Big boys also listen to their mothers."

You're not my mother.

"Well, that nasty dog of yours won't sneak into your room anymore."

Bobby looked up at her, his eyes wide. Her smile grew bigger. Her lips bright red. Her teeth were large. Her eyes were cold, colder than ice.

Very sharp teeth.

Bobby began to tremble violently, and didn't stop until the ambulance arrived. He then began to scream, and didn't stop screaming until three days later when his throat grew too bloody and raw to make noise any longer.

BLOOD AND OCHRE

by

Thomas Barczak

> *"I love the smell of fallen leaves, a musty ochre on winter's eve."*

The press of the ochre left a tingle beneath his skin. It always did – the press of the paint across the canvas, like a second skin, like an afterthought of emotion or a premonition of something better yet to come.

Grant leaned back against the other easel to keep from falling. His legs hurt again, to the point where they'd already gone numb hours ago. He didn't really feel them, only the solid cold ghost-like pain that if he wasn't careful would settle too deep in his soul and never be removed.

But, he'd never been an optimist at heart. Had he?

Until he met her.

Her eyes, almost finished, already they summoned him. Subtle pools of incense – an offering made only for him in the silent moments of the night as he worked on her. This moment in particular, when the pain meds had worn off but the rest of the city hadn't yet woken, when only the buzzing of the street lights offered solace to anyone else.

But with her, he would never be alone.

And he was almost finished with her.

The beautiful Allysandra – introduced to him for a portrait by her father. Money meant nothing to him, only fear of his name, which he never needed to say.

After he brought her, her father stayed and watched them.

Grant shuddered and smiled. He'd tried, oh God he'd tried, to relax then as he'd gone through his normal routine, the bait and talk that he did with every new model that he did just to get them to relax – to trust him. But the truth was he'd needed to feel safe more than she did. He could feel her father's eyes on him. He could taste his displeasure on his tongue. She knew this. Oh God, she knew it. She'd been there herself. So she did. She helped him relax. She helped her father relax to the point where with a seminal grunt, he had walked away. Only the terse rap when he'd come to pick her up later that evening, said anything, and the brown envelope filled with cash.

Grant wiped his brow and eyes. He winced from the sting of thinner mixed with sweat. But it woke him up, just a little bit more, so he could finish her, so he could have her again.

The corners of her mouth turned up in the sputtering neon.

*

"You like watch me?" Allysandra whispered, the corners of her painted mouth never even moving on the canvas. But they didn't need to.

"Yes," Grant answered like he always did to his work, to no one but himself, and this time, to the vision of Allysandra there that held him.

His brush traced the faintest wash of shadow beneath her lips. She was – he was – almost done.

"My father watched you, watching me."

Her lips were full, and musing. It's what she was, wasn't she – his muse – his siren.

"But not anymore, da?"

"Da," Grant smiled. A nervous grin pulled at his lips.

He imagined the same falling across hers. Knowing. Tempting. Strong.

"I like you watching me," Allysandra purred.

He pushed up the nose of his glasses with the end of his brush. It trembled, "I can't help myself but look at you. I couldn't get you out of my head. It's why I had to make you again."

"Da," Allysandra said, and smiled.

*

Grant woke wet. His clothes hung from his skin like moss. The blur of his apartment shifted as he felt for his glasses beneath the couch. The night still breathed in through the open warehouse window casting papers about him.

He could barely make out the time on his watch. He had only been asleep for an hour.

The soft glow of his lover's flesh stared back at him from just beyond his sight. Just beyond his vision. Scrambling, he found his glasses and thrust them upon his face. His heart pounded when he saw her – his Allysandra – stepping toward him.

She knelt beside him. The supple scrape of her skin across his coarse fingertips as he reached for her. She touched his face. Her lips parted as she leaned down to him.

"You complete me," she said.

"Da," Grant whispered as her lips enclosed his.

*

Flakes of ochre settled like fallen leaves on her father's blood where it had pooled under the closet door.

Her father had come back just like he'd told him to. Angry, enraged, confused, her father had come, unable to let the painter get away with knowing something he shouldn't, couldn't have known about his daughter, his beautiful Allysandra, who he'd killed in a drunken jealous rage only the night before.

But last night, it was her father – her Bugimen – who didn't get away, and as his anger crumbled into shame, even his tears had wept for him.

Grant dropped his crutches against the chair, beside the hasty bag he'd just packed but discarded.

Beneath him the sirens of the city called to him in songs of red and blue.

He strode out the front door as the heavy tread of feet gathered up the stairs, and wondered, sometimes even when you can bring them back, if there are some dreams that are better left dead.

THE TESTAMENT OF TUFF

by

C. Dean Andersson

Well, now, yessir, happened one time I was a-drivin' on this little ole blacktop road way back in sum trees just a lookin' fer sumthin' to kill if'n God went an'toll me to when I found me this pup what'd been runned over, fulla fear an'pain, yippin 'n' cryin' sumthin' awful an' a-tryin' to pull hisself along, trailin' a big old smear o'blood 'n' stinkin' guts on that hotter'n bejezus 'n hell July road. Had me a mind to kill the pup an' put 'im outta his misery, but his pup's eyes said he was a wantin' to live pitiful bad. Nosir, never seen me more a look o'wantin' to live, not even in the eyes o'folks what I'd kilt fer God. An' God He didn't tell me to kill that there pup, neither, so I up an' hurried him to a Vet what figured he'd kill the pup, but I said, "You kill that there pup an' I'm a-gonna kill you back." So's after he'd gone an' worked on the pup sum, that little feller went an' pulled hisself through. Even got to kinda walkin' later on. Champ's what I started up a-callin' him, 'cause I figured he'd fought the big fight an' won. Then, yessir, I cried me sum tears when Champ up an' died. He weren't never right inside, I don't reckon. But we had us a couple o'good old years there when God never toll me to kill nuthin' else. Yessir, lotsa times we'd be a-watchin' shows what were funny on the TV, an' I'd get me to laughin' an' Champ he'd get to barkin'. Good ole times. An' a person I knowed toll me he figured Champ were a gift from God, witch I

figured were trew, 'cause God He were just a-thankin' me fer all the
killin' I'd done fer Him from a way back. So, well, yessir, then after
that an' then I went an' got myself borned again on the Death Row,
'cause I went an' saw God after them folks kilt me, an' God He said
He'd put me back to life if'n I'd do sum more killin' fer Him, witch
weren't much to ask. So's I said fine or jim dandy an 'God He put me
back to life in a new set o'bones an' the flesh what covered 'em. Well,
now, nosir, that there new body o'mine weren't much to crow about.
Been dead a bit. But it worked purty good an' it weren't in no derned
prison. But how come folks don't understan' this killin' thing none?
Everthin' what's alive's a-gonna be dead, an' decidin' when sumthin'
what's alive's gonna be dead makes a person special. Figured that's
why God went an' picked on me to do sum killin' fer Him way back
when an' now agin, 'cause I'd kilt me enuff to be showin' Him I were
purty dern special. But I found out purty soon there'd been lotsa
special folks what God'd felt kindly on, 'cause purty soon I weren't
alone by no long shot, an' alla us were wantin' to do sum killin' fer
God. An' by holy hanna in a hoppity pond we meant to dern well do
it, yesir, I tell you what, an' so we went to doin' the rome 'ro'nd a-
lookin' fer folks what weren't special enuff to've had the life put back
in 'em, an' when we found us one, we'd kill 'em an' gnaw on 'em a
little, 'cause God toll me it were okay, we had to eat sumthin'. But
sum started in gnawing on the brains o'them what they kilt to try an'
get more smarts fer their own selfs, but God toll me His Commando
Numero-Ewno was Don't Go Eatin' No Dern Brains, witch He was
wantin' me to spread the Word 'bout, witch was so's He could use
what were left o'them what we kilt later on, 'cause He had Him lotsa
special souls waitin' in line what needed new sets o'bones an' the flesh
what covered 'em. Now, yessir, when we found us a buncha folks hole
up sumwhere or sum other we'd have us a hoot 'n' holler o' a time a-
killin' an' gnawin' on 'em fer God 'fore doin' the rome 'ro'nd, lookin'
fer more, an' them holed up folks'd go an' fight us sumtimes an' what
not but we didn't go an' pay it much nevermind, 'cause we were a

workin' fer God, so's we'd just keep a comin' till we had 'em dead an' gnawed on. But, yessir, God did figure I was a might e'specialler than others, oh, I reckon, 'cause after we'd been a killin' fer Him fer a bit He went an' said in my head, witch were how He'd always went an' talked to me, don't ya know, "Tuff," witch is what he'd stated up a-callin' me, "go an' write Me a Testament 'bout how things have been a-goin' along, an' put down My Commando Numero-Ewno 'bout not eatin' no brains, even tho they got 'em a good taste but won't make you no smarter if'n your new bones an' the flesh what covers 'em weren't smart to start out with, an' like that there." Nossir, yep, 'cause that there body He'd put me in was a-getting' a-little on the used up side, them maggots inside o'me a wigglin' 'round a-causin' a big dern powerful itchin' alla the time, so's I weren't as good at a walkin' an' killin' as I'd been an' already stopped stumblin' on the rome 'ro'ne lookin fer folks to gnaw on. So, started in a-puttin' these here werds down so's others could go an' see 'em if'n they had 'em enuff brains left to want to. Nosir, I weren't sure as shootin' I could go an' do this here writin' thing till I started in a doin' 'er, but I dern sure went an' tried 'cause God He said others what he'd made e'special couldn't think good as me. Toll me the one what'd owned the bones an' the flesh what covered 'em 'fore me were a real smart cookie what'd knowed how to write sum real good stuff 'n' things so's folks'd give 'er money fer it, an' her brains weren't so gone when I moved in I couldn't use 'em sum. Now, yessir, had me sum trouble spellin' these here werds when I went 'n' started out, but God He said I'd do fine or jim dandy once I got to rollin'. An' God He's always right. So, yessir, fer landee-lay till them chickens come home an' sum cows too, I reckon, that there's why I went an 'put down these here werds, so's other special folks what has 'em brains enuff left to know what God toll me to go an' tell 'em could do 'er. But me I'm used up purty good now, so if'n you'd take what's left o'me an' gnaw on me an' sip up a little o'my cold juice what used to be blood an' go an' put sum hole in my head an' gnaw my brains a bit, I'm bein' ready to go an' givie up my holy as hanna in a hoppity pond ghost. God He's a-gonna put me back to life anyways in sum new bones an' the flesh what covers 'em, He toll me, so I'm a-gonna keep on a-comin' back to gnaw on folks what God wants to make e'special. Come on! Now! I'm ready to go! Get you to gnawin' on me quick! An' don't go forgettin' God says this time don't you go sparin' my dead dern maggoty brains! 'Cause...

NIGHT OF THE BETTYS

by

Beverly A. Hale

Paul hated little old people. Hated them with a passion. Especially little old ladies.

Not his own mother, Dolores, of course, but the rest of them – all crumpled and blue-haired and creaking around in their damn wheelchairs.

And he loathed having to run the gauntlet of those little old ladies at the Forest Glade Rest Home just to get to his mom's room at the end of a long hall that stank of powder and piss and death and disinfectant.

It was like they sensed him coming. Like vultures… waiting.

Especially the Bettys.

He really, really hated the Bettys. The home was full of Bettys – thirty or more. There were four of them on his mother's hallway alone. The nurses joked about it. They were all different nationalities, and yet there was a sameness about them that gave him the creeps every time any of them came near him. The four on his mother's hall were the worst.

The nurses said they used to play bridge together and visit and tell stories. That time was now past, and all they did was lurk about the ward like ancient predators.

First he'd hear the squeak of their wheelchairs, like rats in the walls, creak, creak, <u>creak</u>. Then they'd call out to him, "Paauuullll.

Paul." Their voices like dried-up wells, cracking, sucking all the mois-ture from the air and from him. Then they'd appear in the doorways to watch him with sharp, cold, hungry eyes. No matter what day he arrived, what time he tried to sneak down the hall, there were the Bettys. Waiting.

Sometimes he skipped days or even a week between visits. Just to avoid the Bettys. But guilt over leaving his mother alone at the rest home always made him return.

And no one seemed to notice how bizarre they were, except him.

The nurses told him that the Bettys were just lonely because they had no visitors themselves. They said the Bettys liked him because he was a good son who always visited his mother, even though she hardly ever recognized him.

But Paul thought it was something else. Something he didn't want to think about too much. Something unnatural and unclean.

Today he'd almost sprinted down the hallway, trying to get to the safety of his mother's room before they could pin him like a bug on a board with their eyes.

Creaaaakkkkk, "Pauullllll. Paul." One by one the Bettys ap-peared in their doorways.

Each of them wore a bandage. One had her arm in a sling, an-other had her shoulder bound over a wad of bloodied cotton, the third had her hand dressed and the last wore a turban of gauze.

Paul skidded into his mother's room to find her also bandaged. Her neck was packed with sterile pads and taped from her chin to her collarbone. Paul ran to her side, "Mom!"

She never even looked away from the game show running silently on the TV.

"Mom, are you all right?"

He gingerly moved her head, pushing back the lank gray hair to inspect the dressings. He peeled back the tape and gauze pads to see an open wound with what looked like teeth marks.

Then he snatched up the call button and mashed it, cursing under his breath. His mother ignored him.

"Can I help you?" It was Missy, one of the aides.

"What the hell happened to my Mother!?"

"I'll be right there." Missy appeared in the doorway a few moments later. She smiled brightly.

"How did my mother get hurt? No one called *me*."

Missy reddened, "We were just going to call you. Mrs. Downy is perfectly fine now. Everything's been taken care of. We just had a problem with one of the patients. Mr. James was a new transfer to our facility. We weren't told he had... behavior problems." She went to his mother's bed and straightened her bedcovers, plumped up the pillows behind her. His mom ignored her. Missy patted the woman's hand gently.

"Behavior problems? He tried to *eat* my mother!"

The aide began to look a bit queasy, "Let's not exaggerate the situation. I'm sure you don't want to agitate Dolores. Mr. James is already scheduled to go to another more secure facility. Everything is just fine now."

"Everything is *not* fine. You're not getting the *eat my mother* part." Paul tried to hold his mother's hand, but she shook him off and pressed the channel changer. "I want to speak to the administrator."

Now the aide went pale, "I'll bring in the nursing supervisor for you." She grabbed her cell phone from her pocket and pushed a button. "Ms. Walters?" she squeaked. "Mr. Downy is here and would like to speak to you."

"I want to speak to the administrator..." Paul's voice grew louder. "...about you people letting someone *chew on my mother*!"

"It wasn't that bad," Missy shut off the phone, shoved it back into her pocket and straightened the pillows behind his mother's back for the second time. Over the intercom, someone called out "Missy please go to the sunroom."

The aide bolted from the room.

He paced the linoleum floor while he waited. He was somewhere between deciding to sue or call the cops and then sue when Ms. Walters appeared.

"Mr. Downy," she said, holding out a hand. "We were just going to call you when you arrived."

"What kind of place are you *running* here?"

"Please, Mr. Downey – Paul, may I call you Paul?" Ms. Walters smiled patiently at him. "We know how upsetting it can be, but truly, the incident has been handled. Your mother has been treated and is quite unconcerned about this unpleasant but rare occurrence."

"My mother is *unconcerned* because she doesn't *remember* the attack!" Paul backed away from her, "And as for *rare,* the guy chewed on the Bettys, too! You let your new patient make a smorgasbord out of the rest of the people here?" He went to the phone by his mother's bed and lifted the receiver, "I'm calling the cops and the Board of Health."

Ms. Walters darted past him and pushed the off switch, "Please. Wait."

"Why? Is the cannibal patient still hungry?"

"Please. You have to understand; we were told that Mr. James was recovering from a serious injury. The doctor assured us that he would probably be unconscious for at least the first thirty-six hours. In fact," she lowered her voice, "well, we weren't sure Mr. James would actually recover at all. He was so pale and gray when he arrived, we almost sent him directly on to the hospital." Ms. Walters was wringing her hands by now, "But his physician assured us he would be fine and need minimal observation."

"So, you expect me to believe a comatose patient suddenly re-vived and felt well enough to go wandering the halls to *grab a snack* from the Bettys and my mom?" Paul raised an eyebrow.

"I'm afraid that is exactly what happened. We had no idea he would wake up and act out like that," Ms. Walters nodded grimly. "And, actually, he went to your mother's room first. The other ladies were injured while trying to protect your mother from him. They managed to get to a call button so the orderlies were able to get there quickly." She ran a hand through her sensible haircut, "Mr. Downy. it took three large orderlies and a nurse to get him back under control. We had to put double restraints on him. This is totally unprecedented in my twenty years of experience."

Paul took her arm, "He didn't give my mom rabies or something?"

"We transferred him immediately to the psychiatric ward at County General, and are awaiting the results of the lab tests, but it appears he wasn't rabid." She patted his hand, "Let me assure you, Paul, Forest Glen doesn't accept patients with such obvious control issues. We aren't equipped to deal with such things. We are here to help make patients comfortable and secure in their declining days. We were told Mr. James fit into that criterion."

"You were wrong."

"We were misinformed."

Paul allowed himself to be mollified, "You're sure my mother will be all right?"

"Barring something unusual in the lab tests, I'd say your mother will have no ill effects from this unfortunate incident."

"If it happens again…"

"It won't," she countered with a firm voice.

He turned to his mother, who still ignored him in favor of the muted television game show. "Mom, I'll be back to see you tomorrow." He leaned down to hug her, but she moved away and turned her head toward the screen. He sighed and stood up.

"You better take care of her," he warned Walters.

"Of course."

As he left the room, Paul stopped. The Bettys had saved his mother. As much as he disliked them, they had literally saved his mom's life. Damn. Now he'd *have* to be nice to them. He plodded slowly to the first door, "Er, Betty?" He peered in. She sat in her bed staring fixedly at him.

"Paullllll."

"Yep, that's me. Paul. I wanted to, um, thank you and the others for helping my mother."

"Paullllll."

"Yep, still Paul," he blushed and sketched a limp wave. "Well, good-bye now." With that he hastily backed away. From his right he could hear creaks. Spinning around he saw the other three Bettys, edging through the doorways in their wheelchairs. "Hi, ah, ladies. I was coming to thank you all for, uh, for helping Mom. I really appreciate it."

They nodded in chorus and rolled closer, "Paulllll. Good boy."

Okay, they were still creeping him out. He skirted around them, "I have to go. I'll see you tomorrow." With that he almost galloped down the hall, not willing to look back at the Bettys.

Near the lobby area he jogged around a gurney with a patient strapped onto it. The man lay strangely quiet, and if he didn't know better, Paul would have thought the man dead, especially from the stink that hung over the area.

He sped up and shoved through the doors to the outside, not slowing until he reached his car, where he stood panting. The fresh air had never smelled sweeter.

*

The next morning he decided to go back to Forest Glen as soon he finished work. Despite Ms. Walters' assurances, he wanted to make sure Mom was better. However, by the time he finished tying up some loose ends at the office, it was already dark. Paul usually tried to avoid the nursing home at night. Somehow the place seemed more eerie and claustrophobic as the shadows grew longer.

Still, he'd promised his mother.

Though it wasn't like she'd miss him if he didn't show up. She hardly knew he was there when he did visit.

But he had promised. And occasionally – well, rarely – but some-times she did recognize him. They'd even had conversations, of a sort.

So he went.

The lobby was far quieter than he'd expected. No one sat on the front desk. No nurses or attendants hurried across dingy linoleum. But he heard creaking… those damned wheelchairs. They all seemed to be heading his way. It was probably more of those Bettys. A shiver went up his back. He rushed toward his mother's hallway.

The hallway still smelled of old people – disinfectant and death. Holding his nose, Paul breathed through his mouth. Even so, there was a metallic stench that got through and made him gag. Most of the doorways were dark; the elderly usually went to bed early, thank God, so he tiptoed down the hallway.

He paused to one side of a Betty's door and then scooted past as quickly and quietly as a thief. He did the same at each of the other Bettys' doors.

Heaving a sigh of relief when he heard no creaking, he pushed open the door to his mother's room.

She was sitting up in bed, and for once she wasn't glued to the TV. Though she looked a bit grey, she turned to him, sat up straighter in the bed and her eyes lit up, "Paul."

She knew him.

Maybe the new meds were working and she'd gone into some sort of Alzheimer's remission. He almost bounced across the floor as he crossed to her.

His mother opened her arms wide, so he perched on the edge of the bed and bent forward to hug her. She hugged him back, an occur-rence so rare that he almost pulled back before relaxing to lean into the embrace. He sighed happily.

"It's so good to see you, Mom," he whispered.

"Good," she answered and tightened her arms around him. She smelled a bit sour and metallic.

As she rested her head on his shoulder he heard creaking behind him. He tried to pull away so he could look, but his mother held him tightly.

"Paullllllll," four voices called in quiet gravelly tones. He turned as best he could and looked around his mother's head. The Bettys, and behind them, all the rest of the Bettys from the home were rolling slowly forward, "Good boy." There was blood around their mouths.

"Paullll," his mother said and licked his neck.

Paul recoiled but couldn't break her grip. The creaking grew nearer, louder.

His mother bit into his throat. Searing pain shot through his body as his life blood began to rush from his veins. One by one, the Bettys joined the feast. As the blackness began to take him, he heard the voice of his mother one last time.

"Good boy."

JACK THE RAPTOR

by

Chris Morris

> *What god, or fiend, or spirit of the earth,*
> *Or monster turned to a manly shape,*
> *Or of what mould or mettle he be made,*
> *What star or fate soever govern him, [...]*
> – Christopher Marlowe, *Tamburlaine the Great, Pt 1*

"Jaaaccckkk, Jaaaccck," came the call, echoing over Whitechapel's sixty-two bawdy houses, bouncing off cobblestones, resounding along twisty lanes in darkest night.

"Jaaaccckkk, Jaaaccck," Again. Whores and hell-hounds paused about their business, for they'd heard that call before. Before harlots were found eviscerated with long claw marks scoring faces, one with heart missing, one with kidneys torn away; their guts and sex spread all about the alleys.

Mary Ann Nichols, Annie Chapman, Elizabeth Stride, Catherine Eddowes and Mary Jane Kelly: every bawd working Whitechapel knew their names, and where they'd died, and how. Add injury to shame, and fear chokes minds and hearts: throats severed, abdomens ripped, (except for Stride). One or two sure slashes to the neck, for each and all, to send these strumpets straight to hell...

"Jaaaccckkk, Jaaaccck."

Lanes emptied faster than a chamber pot spilled from a window.

"Jaaaccckkk, Jaaaccck." Right in front of me, a wild call to chill the soul.

I was the last boy out on High Street; I knuckled my eyes. Blinked. Looked again.

Before me was a beast, half bird, half lizard, six feet long and not three feet high. It sighted me, raised up high, balanced on its long straight tail and two big-clawed hind feet, and stared. Tilted its head. And cooed.

"Jaaaccckkk, Jaaaccck," this thing said, much softer and took one bold step toward me. Two.

Its front legs were short and feathered, its hands three-clawed. Behind it lay a carcass: no telling what those gristly bones had been before this scavenger found them.

Luminous eyes held me with their gaze. This lizardy bird was beautiful, pinions spreading.

Then it changed its shape – or seemed to change, still coming at me.

Now a boy my age approached, in a velvet cloak. For a moment more this boy-thing still had its long straight tail, stiffly lashing. A boy with a tail? Not even in Whitechapel. Any whore who bore a long-tailed child would have strangled it and thrown it in the street.

Then that tail was gone and in its stead was a completely beautiful boy, small, with feathery hair.

"Jaaaccckkk, Jaaaccck," said he, so softly.

"Jack? Your name is Jack?" I hazarded, backing away a bit, for he was still coming on: "M'name is Mac. Pleased to meet." What else could a poor boy say? Nothing on my person was worth having, so this other boy hadn't robbery in mind. And his cloak alone, fine and feathered like cut-silk velvet, was worth a month's wage to a boy as poor as I.

No tail now. But his head still the cocked head, and coming closer.

Then: claws on three long fingers. Massive claws on wide-spread feet: now you see 'em, now you don't. In a blink of an eye, boy and lizardy bird melted together, came apart, and were all boy once more.

Still, behind him was that carcass; on his face was a smear of gore. He saw me look at it and wiped his lips, "Jaaaacckk, Jaaaacckk…" Soft and plaintive.

"Y'can't talk? Or are ye daft?" My buttocks hit a building wall: no further retreat possible. So: "Let's walk a ways together, Jack. Jack and Mac are safer on these nights, with bloody murderers about, than either one of us alone."

Some hell-hounds, drunken soldiers, turned into our alleyway just then.

Jack puffed up, and changed once more, his wingy little arms spread wide, and charged them: "Jaaaaccckkk! Jaaaaccck!"

And those sots that would've run me through for fun or spite turned and ran as if they'd seen ghosts come avenging. Jack chased them, screeching his name in a voice to curdle blood. And took wing. And scored the hindmost, all down the back, with a big hind claw as they rounded the corner.

Then did this apparition flutter to the cobbles, and peer about, bating. And stalk, claws full extended on hands and feet, back to me: *clack, clack, clack.*

When the lizardy bird was no more than three foot from me, it took to the air again, leaping at my chest.

I caught it in my arms, thinking to wrestle it to the death. But it retracted its biggest, most fearsome claws and nuzzled its head against my chest and began to purr its name once more: "Jaaaacccckkk, Jaaaaccck."

So I held it, frozen in fright, and then realized: it was young; it was lonely; it needed a friend. And it was, clearly, the best friend a boy abroad in Whitechapel could have of a dark and tumultuous night with murderers on the loose and drunken men out looking to slay any who might be hacking whores to bits in the city.

And that's how I met Jack the Raptor.

When we're alone, he doesn't make me see him as a boy. He's no taller than my hip, but thrice that long. I made him realize it wasn't good to slash girls to death; that we'd be better off poaching deer and the occasional calf.

So long ago, it seems now. Jack never looks a day older, and protects me every day in every way.

We travel, as it's safer. I grew from boy to man, and he grew... more cautious under my hand.

The murders of loose women in Whitechapel stopped, so it's said, right about the time we left London.

A good thing, all be told. The world changes, day to day, but Jack never changes – except when he wants to seem a boy, or a man – which he's done since I grew up.

He never says much, not even when he's boy or man, just "Jaaaccckkk, Jaaaccck," but if he could speak clearly, what wondrous tales he'd tell. He sits in my lap when he's replete, and I've had all I need to eat, and retracts those big front claws, kneading them against my knee.

So safe we be, together... forever mayhap – since it's many years since first we met, far beyond the day I should have dried up and curled up and died of age and ague. We've traveled far, and seen such sights as would amaze the bawds in High Street.

Something's magic about my Jack, but only a fool looks too closely at such a friend.

Now we have this place, a little farm that borders woodland, a sea away from where we met. And all was well with us, until *she* came by one day.

Her name's Nell. She came and no hint dissuaded her: she stayed. This uninvited guest upset Jack, who's chased her once away, and twice away, and through the woods and into town today. With his wings spread wide and his claws extended, screeching, he's flown at her too many times: "Jaaaccckkk, Jaaaccck," or maybe "Baaaccckkk, Baaaccck," he'd call.

What am I to do? Jack's been my only friend, the partner of my heart, since earliest days. We've fought our share of battles, true, but only against brigands, bounty-hunters, and those black of heart seeking to blame Jack for their own marauding.

Sometimes Jack gets hungry for a tussle, to take down prey with a fighting heart. But when that's all done and those who've seen us – seen him and thought to kill him or trap him – rest cold in death, off we go, to somewhere else. There to start again, to live again, to hunt again, to eat again and sleep again without one ear pricked for the king's men or the vigilantes or the heroes out to catch us. Sometimes, though, those Whitechapel days come back to Jack and make him hungry.

But Nell came and Jack was right: we should have sent her packing, tossed her out on her fine white rump. Now it's too late. Damage done, plans unstrung.

These days, if Jack's nature were unveiled, life would be a horror for us both. And short.

She's in the town and Jack is… where?

Not here.

Not today.

Out comes my coat. Out comes my knife. Out come my boots. Then, ready to fight if needs must, it's time to go seeking Jack, bring him home. And her? If she has enticed my Jack to harm, then her fate's made by her own hand.

White rump, soft lips, woman's musk and all her charms come dancing before my eyes as I pull open the cabin door to do what I must.

Outside, a big man stands, in a heavy slicker, with broad shoulders and a grim square jaw.

"What?" I need to know.

"Jaaaccckkk, Jaaaccck," says he, plaintively, looking at the knife stuck in my belt. "Baaaccckkk, Baaaccck," says he, softer still. And "Maaaccc, Maaaccc."

The slicker shivers into feathers; the jaw grows its fangs; the broad shoulders are pinions; claws clack forward and back.

Into my arms Jack launches himself, and nuzzles my throat.

The smell of blood is on his snout, his feathers; sticky and damning. Nell's blood? Or gore from some doe in the woods?

But I don't ask what I don't want to know. Ever.

"Time to go?" I ask Jack.

Luminous eyes catch mine. "Maaaccc, Maaaccc," Jack says my name again, clear as a bell tolling.

So now we must run, leave this place, ahead of the law; of any mob coming from the town – outrun them or outfight them.

For there is another law: survival, a law that Jack knows better than they.

I can hear pursuers, I fancy, as we make away, with their dogs and their shouts and their bloodlust.

But Jack and I will be fine; fine in another place; fine when this tale ends: bloodlust is something we both understand. Together we learned young and learned well how to let the wild heart loose, free the raptor in our souls.

On any night. On any day. When the battle joins, and feathers cover me; when my teeth turn to fangs and my long claws clack where fingers were before; then do I want only Jack the Raptor by my side.

Racing through the wood, Jack can't resist: he throws back his head and screeches at the dappled sky above: "Jaaaccckkk, Jaaaccck."

My pulse pounding, I throw back my own head and answer in kind: "Maaaccc, Maaaccc."

FAILURE TO COMPLY

by

Michael H. Hanson

"A deal is a deal." – Ferengi Rule of Acquisition #16

The feeding was a great success, but he had expected no less. Bleeding through walls of paint, plaster, sheetrock, concrete rebar, and brick facing, he quickly exited out into the open. It was a clear, moon-lit night in the heart of winter and the streets were silent at this late hour.

The victim had been so very tasty. A terrified divorcee, middle-aged, alone, half of a lifetime of regrets, cradling a cheap bottle of booze, and cursing all that is good and precious in the world. No, it did not take a renunciation of any religious deity to grant him access to this one nor appeals to any devil. The tasty one had already con-demned herself, her cursing of things precious just the latest in a series of poor decisions that had led to this point. The true spiritual manna that flows invisibly through the arteries of all humanity is a much more complex and shy miracle than most ever realize. Its variables, not unlike his monstrous form, do not follow any path of tortured logic. No popular biblical tale or scientific reasoning can explain his exis-tence.

Rising high into the night sky he lays bare his senses. He wishes to feed a second and third time if possible. With luck he will return to this prey, perhaps next month. Did he forget to mention? He is not a killer. He does not leave corpses in his wake, at least, not literally. This woman, having rejected her own humanity and the goodness of her own heart, he left in a languor the direct result of his having encouraged her despair in order to feed upon her innermost grief. Often these humans commit suicide if he feeds too strongly. Not that he cares, and it certainly is not something that could ever be traced to him, being non-human and incorporeal. But there are times when even he feels lazy, and does not wish to search so hard for those drowning in melancholy.

Bo... Man, a distant whisper leaked into his consciousness.

Using his supernatural senses to examine the surrounding several miles of open air, he detected no presence. Still, this half-imagined sound sent a chill through his misty form. Perhaps this was not a good hunting ground for the rest of the evening.

With the smallest of exertions he quickly shifted into The Path, that sub-space lightless realm he used to travel instantaneously between any two points upon the Earth. It is a painful plane of existence bound by disturbing, reality-altering forces, and one he frequented only when necessary. A split second later he was gone.

*

The unnamed incarnation of dread and hopelessness reappeared within reality above a small clearing in Somalia, Africa. It was still evening, and a homeless tribe of starving families lay sleeping around a dying fire. During past famines he had supped mightily upon the spiritual pain that accompanied so many dying of starvation, but tonight there was a rancid smell of hope drifting through the dreams of these sleeping natives.

A supernaturally rapid reconnaissance across the entire country showed that this same sense of well-being ran rampant throughout the long-suffering population. Recent cease fires among tribal factions, and massive humanitarian aid were finally having their positive effect upon this war torn landscape.

Bo... Man, a flicker of thought crossed his mind.

Unease sifted through his incorporeal form and he instinctively slipped into The Path.

*

He hovered above the islands of Japan. Over a year ago the earthquake off the coast of Tohoku had provided a seemingly unending feast of extreme anxiety and naked fear. The tsunami, and even better, the eventual failure of the Fukushima nuclear power reactor planted the seeds of multiple nightmares among the stalwart population.

It had been months since he'd last fed among this island nation. He'd been called away by the delicious aromas of war and bloodshed to feed amidst the many revolutions that had spread throughout the Middle-East. In the last couple of months the revolutions had fizzled out and the world entered a strange lethargy in its horrors and despairs. Yes, all the evils and crimes that humanity breeds were still in full swing, but it felt to him that some strange new shift was spreading through the planet-wide populations, some horrible sense of maturity, and new respect for life.

Hovering close to the concrete encased Fukushima plant, he could instantly sense that all the surrounding populace was no longer in the grip of terror. For some reason, their fatalism had been replaced with an unpalatable optimism.

This will not do, he thought to himself.

And then, almost as if he had expected it, the beginnings of a voice echoed in the air.

Bo... Man.

This time it was louder than before, and the words were becoming more pronounced, and they sounded like a short sentence being spoken over an unstable radio communication, with the transmission fading in and out.

He focused all his power in all directions, but could detect no opponent of any kind. Not that he'd faced any such force for many millennia... this stray thought sent a trickle of memory through him that he quickly rejected.

Acknowledging his own fear, he dove into The Path.

*

He hovered above a brothel in a slum in Leningrad, Russia. The east European sex slave trade had its heart in this dank neighborhood, and the quality of suffering was a veritable smorgasbord on this lean night.

Bo... Man the mental voice projected louder than ever. This time the proximity of frightening power was manifesting much too close for comfort. Memories of many enemies, strange beings with various powers, usurpers who thought they could infringe on his feeding grounds, flooded into his mind. Most he had defeated and destroyed. A few he had fought to a standstill, and then simply outlived them. But there was one, a creature unlike anything that had ever manifested on this jewel of a planet. If it had returned, than it was time to engage his long delayed scheme, and to do so would require as much power as he could consume in the few moments he had left.

Diving like a bird of prey the shadow creature shot silently through walls, and fed strongly upon the sleazy horror and depravity all around.

He could feel the thing following him in unrelenting pursuit.

Bo... Man, it became a shout in the ether. Closer.

From room to room, and ramshackle apartment building to wooden shack, he flew, diving through the forms of kidnapped and enslaved teenage girls, forcibly injected with heroin to gain their dependence, and only given nourishment after acquiescing to the most deplorable and sickening of sex acts and Sado-masochistic tortures. One of mankind's oldest terrors and banes gorged on these depravities as it led a phantom pursuer on a wild chase.

One young woman, a blonde college student from Norway who had lost all hope, was suffering through a brutal gang rape as she caught a brief glimpse of two shadow entities flying into and out of the sleazy warehouse that was her prison. Thinking they were angels, and feeling a small moment of hope, she reached out and grabbed a hunting knife jutting from one rapist's boot. Before anyone could react she shoved the blade into her throat, ending her nightmare.

In a matter of minutes he had glutted himself on the negative energies of the hellish neighborhood and knew he had to play his endgame. Rising suddenly upward, through the roof of an abandoned church that was now a brothel for pedophiles, he waited for the briefest moments to make sure his pursuer had not fallen behind.

BO...

He shot into The Path...

*

...and exited beneath a star filled sky. In all directions lay endless wastelands. It was the heart of Siberia.

Knowing what was to follow almost immediately, he shot downward to hover within a small circle of standing stones, each about six feet tall, and bearing no markings.

BOOGEY MAN!

The shout was a ripping pain throughout his ectoplasmic mind.

The pursuing dark cloud, a miasma of boiling, frightening power, descended from the heavens to settle upon the ground a mere dozen yards from the miniature Stonehenge.

I've come for my payment, Boogey Man.

The pursuing black mass instantly contracted, and in moments transformed into the figure of a tall, slim Caucasian man wearing a black fedora and a long, black trench coat.

The foul, nearly invisible creature hovering over the stones dropped to the ground and slowly coalesced into a roughly humanoid shape, wearing a dark brown robe with large hood keeping his face in shadow. Scaly, claw-like hands extended beyond the sleeves. His feet were covered with slimy, wriggling snake-like creatures. An oily mist slowly leaked out of the cowl.

The clean-cut, black-haired man with the fedora hat spoke.

"It is time."

"No," the Boogey Man replied with a voice that sounded like a thousand worms crawling on a corpse, "you will not compel me… Salesman."

The Salesman adjusted his dark trench coat and smiled, revealing a shark-like grin filled with perfect white teeth with the exception of a single shiny gold left incisor.

"We had a deal, my friend," the Salesman said, "and surely you know that one cannot break a contract with me."

The Salesman walked forward as the Boogey Man backed up against one of the stones on the other side of the circle.

"Come, come," the Salesman said happily, "your wonderful robe, which you've worn for over eight thousand years, has been a blessing to you. Confess. Without it you would forever be an incorporeal thing stuck in the land of dreams and the sub-conscious, but with it you can manifest as a solid being, albeit for a limited number of minutes at a time. And over the ages it has allowed you to infiltrate and directly, physically, interact with humanity. And ohhhh how you have enjoyed terrifying the sheep of society, Boogey Man…"

The Salesman walked into the center of the stones and stared pointedly at the the foul creature standing before him. "It was a very wise trade on your part," the Salesman said, "but now my terms have come due… I'm here to collect."

A short, creepy chuckle emitted from the blackness inside the Boogey Man's cowl.

"Salesman," the Boogey Man spat, "vaunted hero of humanity and self-professed demi-god from beyond, Trickster and Trader, you think I fear you? I know your weaknesses fool, and now you are mine."

The Boogey Man leaped outside the circle of stones. Instantaneously a beam of oily, glistening yellow light emanated from his cowled head and struck one of the stones. The sickening energy then leapt from stone to stone until the Salesman was surrounded. A moment later the energy rose and became a glistening dome over the circle.

"It is a globe, Salesman," the Boogey Man said, "you cannot escape through the earth below."

"You're making a big mistake," the Salesman said.

"Bah, I've studied you over the years like a scientist does an ant," the Boogey Man said, "and I know what happened in Poland during WWII. Oh, surprised are you? Yes, I saw you captured, nullified for years, trapped against your will, imprisoned and helpless. And all it took was a handful of black diamond dust from a distant hell."

"And these standing stones?" the Salesman asked.

"Hah," the Boogey Man laughed, "props I created a few decades ago. Each contains one of the dreaded black gems, and now, powered by me, they exert a force as great as that which bound you and kept you under the Nazis' thumbs for the majority of that delicious war."

"But I *did*, escape," the Salesman smiled.

"Only by a quirk of fate," the Boogey Man said, "yes, I watched from a distance. When I am through here, this site will be buried deep in the Earth, where you will be incarcerated in this bubble for a million years."

"So long?" the Salesman asked.

"I infused these dark diamonds with the majority of my power," the Boogey Man said, "a millennium of shame, and fear, and despair that I have long and heartily supped on, and hoarded, and all of it injected into this trap. And now, with you restrained, I am free to feed as I have never before. The Sha'Daa is coming... and without you to oppose it, I will feast upon an entire world overrun by multiple apocalypses."

"There is only one minor flaw in your disgusting proposition," the Salesman smiled.

"Your bravado is pitiable," the Boogey Man said, "have you no other final words on this auspicious occasion? No? Then tell me, quickly before I dismiss you from history. What is the small error in my brilliant plan?"

"Your entire scheme," the Salesman said as his entire form began to emit a bright blue light, "is predicated on a falsehood." The yellow light grew in incandescence until it seemed a small sun was being born in the wilderness.

"You are trapped," the Boogey Man yelled, "just like you were well over half a century ago."

"Had I chosen to exert my true power during those fateful years," the Salesman said as the blue light became even brighter, and the yellow walls of the surrounding sphere began to warp and shimmer wildly, "I could have breached that trap as a human would a wet paper bag."

"Then, why didn't you?" the Boogey Man gasped in shock.

"Because," the Salesman said, "I had no desire to annihilate the heart of Europe. And in case you've forgotten, after leading me out here on this merry chase, we are now hundreds of miles from any human being."

"Noooo," the Boogey Man screamed as the yellow sphere of power exploded in a maelstrom of expanding energies the equal of a dozen, modern nuclear detonations.

*

As the millions of tons of matter and debris rained down upon the earth, the Boogey Man slowly came to his senses. The partly incorporeal nature of his present form had saved him from the majority of the explosion, yet still, he had received hundreds of psychic wounds that would take centuries to heal. His brown robe and cowl were mostly unharmed, with only a minor tear here and there to betray the recent cataclysm. In moments, the Boogey Man realized he was sitting in a massive crater, half a mile deep and almost two miles across. The sound of crunching earth to his left caught his attention.

"No," the Boogey Man said in horror, struggling to stand up, and too weak to slip into The Path, "I, I won't. I can't, not that."

Appearing from the surrounding dust like some dark avenger, the Salesman strode forward without pity. He grabbed the Boogey Man with his right hand, and then pulled open his black trench coat with his left.

"A promise taken is a promise sold," the Salesman laughed maniacally, "and a bargain's a bargain... no matter how old."

With a Herculean twist of his wrist, the Salesman shoved the Boogey Man, headfirst, into his trench coat's inner left pocket.

Like a miniature black hole, the small fabric opening in the Salesman's clothing pulled at the ancient monster, crushing the Boogey Man down into a fraction of his original mass and size, dragging him down, endlessly down, deep into a bottomless fall, forever dropping for all eternity, in absolute darkness, surrounded and jostled by innumerable objects, fellow chess pieces in the Salesman's ten millennia long penance and battle against that most formidable of Earth's adversaries, the forty-eight-hour long holocaust known as The Sha'Daa.

The Salesman turned and walked toward the crater's edge. For all the horror and terror the Boogey Man had projected into the history of mankind over thousands of years, he was still, in the end, a minor annoyance in the greater scheme of things. Fearsome, pitiless monsters and Hell-spawn beyond the imagination of humanity were even now slavering and waiting in the cracks and shadows between dimensions and worlds, waiting to commit unholy atrocities all across the Earth. The time when they would breach the barriers protecting this planet was fast approaching. The nightmare known as The Sha'Daa was near.

The Salesman shivered, then disappeared.

SHADOW OF A DOUBT

by

Larry Atchley, Jr.

Out of the corner of my eye, I saw the shadow move.

Shadows shouldn't move on their own, I thought.

Thinking, at first, that someone had broken into the house, I grabbed the pump action shotgun I kept by the bed and racked a shell into the chamber with a loud cha-chunk. I searched through the house, with the tactical light mounted under the barrel spot-lighting every corner and closet of each room. I turned on all the lights. I found no one.

That's weird. I could've sworn I saw something.

I checked the front and back doors, and all the windows, making sure they were locked. Finding nothing amiss, I chalked it up to being tired. I put the shotgun back and got ready for bed.

As I walked from the bathroom to the bed, I saw it again... just a hint of movement in the kitchen. It looked like someone dressed all in black and wearing a long coat. I ran into the kitchen and flipped on the light. Again, no one there.

What the hell is going on, I thought. Am I seeing things? I shook my head and rubbed my eyes.

"I must be working too hard," I said. "It's making me loopy."

Being a biochemist isn't the easiest job in the world, and the hours can suck the life out of you. But it pays the bills nicely at least. Maybe I just need some time off.

I shut off the light in the kitchen and went to bed. I lay down and almost as soon as my head hit the pillow I started to fall asleep.

A sound like loud heavy panting right by my head startled me awake, and just as my eyes snapped open, a dark almost featureless face appeared next to mine.

"Derek!" It yelled at me, and then vanished.

I leaped back across the bed, away from where the face materialized.

"Holy shit!" I exclaimed, my face pale and my heart beating twice its normal pace.

I thought frantically, What the hell was that? Was I dreaming? No, my eyes were open and awake. Dammit, what is wrong with me? Now I'm hallucinating? I think I could really use a drink about now.

I got up, turned the lights on, and tentatively looked around the room to make sure nothing was hiding, ready to jump out at me again. I went into the kitchen, poured myself a double of twelve-year old Irish whiskey, straight, no ice. I drank it down in one gulp.

"Ahhhhhh, yeah that's smooth stuff. Whew."

The warmth of the liquor spread through my throat, chest and stomach quickly. I started to relax all over; the tension in my body eased. My racing heart slowed. I poured another glassful, but drank this one more slowly, savoring it as I mulled over what just happened.

If you asked anybody else they'd say they saw a ghost. I don't believe in that bullshit though. It's just the product of an overactive imagination and too little sleep, that's all. Hell, I'm going to have a couple more drinks and then my mind will be too busy marinating to trick me into seeing stupid shit like that again.

I started to pour more of the golden liquid into the tumbler when I heard the sharp breathing like I'd heard before… this time from behind me.

I spun around, sloshing some of the whiskey out of the glass and onto the floor. I dropped the tumbler when I saw what made the noise. It looked like someone cut out a piece of darkness shaped like a man wearing a hooded floor length coat. The silhouette of shadow rushed across the room stopping just in front of me.

"Believe in me now? Heh, heh, heh, heh," the apparition said in a rough, low, raspy voice. It laughed in my face before disappearing.

I was stunned. I couldn't move. I couldn't scream. I was frozen with terror and scared sober all at once. I finally came back to my senses. I jumped into my sports car, and drove to the nearest hotel checking myself into a room for the night. I slept fitfully, tossing and turning. What if the shadow thing followed me here?

The next morning I woke up exhausted, hungover, and confused. What the hell is in my house?

I thought about some of the TV shows that I'd seen an episode or two of that dealt with unexplained occurrences, paranormal pheno- mena they called it. I watched those shows with the attitude that it was all fake, staged for the cameras to garner big network ratings. I laughed whenever they found 'evidence' of some ghostly voices, or apparitions. It was ridiculous, trying to prove these 'ghosts' were real. It's all just smoke and mirrors, I thought. It was the kind of stuff I never believed in the possibility of existing. At least until now. Now I'd come face to face with something I couldn't explain away. What could I do? I couldn't live in a hotel. I should go back to the house and face this thing. But, I didn't think I could do it alone. Maybe I could find one of those paranormal groups to go into my house, figure out what it was, and tell it go away. I heard they could do stuff like that.

I searched online for a listing of local paranormal investigation groups. I found one in the area. The woman I spoke with said that someone could meet with me at the house right away since this was obviously an urgent case. She took my information.

Maybe I'm just overreacting, but better to let people who have experience with this sort of thing handle it. Besides, I don't think I want to go back in my house alone until I know it's gone.

I went back to the house that evening a few minutes before the team of investigators was supposed to show up. I waited outside in the car, in the driveway, not daring to go near the house. After a while a black van pulled up, followed by a blue four door hatchback car. A logo on the side of the van painted in white letters displayed the team's name: P.I.P.S. – People Investigating Paranormal Stuff.

Well, at least they were professional enough to have a van with a painted logo. I guess that's a good sign. From the van stepped a man and a woman in their mid to late thirties; from the car, a guy who looked to be in his twenties. I got out of my car, as they walked up to introduce themselves.

"Hi, you must be Derek James. I'm Kate, and this is Eric my co-investigator, and Chuck, our equipment tech."

I shook their hands, "Glad to meet you. Thanks for coming out on such short notice."

"We're glad we could come help you deal with whatever you have going on in your home," Eric replied. "We know it isn't easy when you have something you can't explain disrupt your life."

"Yes," I said. "Well I just want to know if you can tell me if I'm crazy or not, I guess," I laughed a dry sort of chuckle, "and if I'm not, then I want whatever is in my house gone."

"We'll do our best to find out what's going on, Mr. James," Kate said.

They went to the back of the van and began unloading hard cases filled with equipment. Letting them into the house, I timidly followed. I looked around, expecting to see the shadowy figure pop up at any moment. Nothing happened. I watched the team move the plastic and metal boxes into the house, as they set up a command center in the large open living room.

"Wow, you guys have a lot of gear," I said. "I thought a lot of that stuff was just for the TV shows."

"Well, Mr. James," Chuck said, "it takes a lot of scientific equipment to capture evidence of paranormal phenomena these days. First, we have to rule out the possibility that it's just something natural occurring that is misconstrued as paranormal. Then we can use whatever evidence we find to support the theory that there may be spiritual or other activity in a location."

"I see," I said. "And what if you *do* find evidence something that isn't normal is really in someone's house?"

"Well, Mr. James," Kate interjected as she walked into the room, "it all depends on how malevolent the entity is behaving. If it's frightening the occupants, or causing bodily harm, then we ask it to stop doing what it's doing, or ask it to leave. Depends on what the occupant wants and how much the entity is willing to cooperate."

"Okay," I said. "Well I just want it gone from here, if you can do that. I never believed in these things until yesterday and I'm not sure I want to believe in them now, but I do know that I want it gone, and I don't want it to come back."

Eric walked up with a case in his hands and added, "We'll have to see what we can find as far as evidence first, and then we'll know better how to deal with it."

They got the command center set up, with a widescreen digital monitor on a folding table and a DVR security camera system hooked up to it. They placed cameras with infrared lights around the house at various places, especially two cameras at different angles of the kitchen and bedroom where the shadow manifested the most. Then they set out handheld digital cameras, voice recorders, and some other stuff I'd seen on TV but didn't remember what they were called. When it was dark outside they made sure every light was off in the house, and then started the investigation. Chuck stayed at the table watching the screen with its views of the different stationary cameras places around the house. Kate and Eric each took a handheld camera and recorder and other gear with them and started to walk through the house together.

"If whatever scared the owner of this house is here, show yourself to us, or make your presence known by talking into this recorder," Eric said.

"Let us know that you are here," Kate added. "You wanted Derek to know that you were here, last night. Did you try to scare him? We aren't scared of you, so you might as well give us a sign that you're here."

From the left side of the living room, a quiet voice rasped, "I'm here."

Derek jumped, backing into the wall of the bedroom.

"Did you hear that?" Eric asked Kate as he pointed his camera into the living room.

"Yeah," Kate said. "Clear as day, I heard it. We should have it on audio too. I'm also getting a big spike on the EMF detector."

"We heard you talk to us," Kate said. "Why are you here?"

Nothing but silence.

Then, from the kitchen, came the sound of loud heavy breathing. Kate and Eric spun around with their cameras pointed in that direction. As they turned around, a shadowy figure ran past them and right by Eric.

"Oh shit," Eric said as he fumbled with the camera, spinning around, and trying to catch the movement of the shadow.

"Did you see that?" He asked Kate.

"Uh huh," She said. "Full bodied shadow person apparition. I've never seen one that well defined or so closely. Mr. James, I think you've got the real deal here."

"Uh, ah, yeah. Well, at least I'm glad I'm not crazy," I said. "Although I think I'd choose crazy over having that thing in my house. Can you get rid of it?"

"We'll do our best, Mr. James," Kate said. "First we'd like to study it a bit longer if you don't mind. We don't get this kind of experience very often you see. Most of our cases turn out to be noisy ventilation ducts, or air in the water pipes. It's very rare to witness a full bodied apparition."

"Have you ever seen one before?" I asked.

"Ah, well, actually no," Eric said.

"I got it on the DVR camera too," Chuck said from the table in the living room.

Just then, I saw the shadow figure rush through the room stopping directly in front of Kate.

"Get out now. This is my house," the shadow form hissed at her face.

Kate stood unmoving, seemingly unfazed by the thing's utterance and appearance before her.

"This is not your house," Kate said. "It belongs to Derek James. He does not want you here. Be gone from this place and never return."

The shadowy form drew back away from her, as if rebuked by her statement.

"No," it said, "*You* will be gone."

It lunged toward Kate and seemed to slide into her body. She dropped the camera and audio recorder, convulsing in place violently. The shadow then left her body. She crumpled to the floor.

"Shit, Kate, are you okay?" Eric rushed to her side.

"What the hell just happened?" yelled Chuck, running from the living room to where Kate lay sprawled on the floor. "On the camera it looked like it went right through her."

Eric kneeled beside her, his hand placed on her side.

"She's not breathing!" Eric said. He put his finger to her throat. "No pulse guys. Holy shit, she's dead. That thing killed her!"

"That… that's not possible," Chuck said. "How the…"

The shadow reappeared, streaked across the room, and stopped in front of Chuck.

Its smooth face was devoid of expression. I couldn't see any lips as it spoke.

"Possible," it said. It then jumped into Chuck, dragging him backward and into the brick wall behind us. They hit hard; Chuck's body slid down the wall to lie unmoving where it landed.

"Dammit!" I yelled. "Do something! You're supposed to be experts at this kind of shit. Can't you stop this thing?"

Eric stood transfixed, looking first at Kate's body, then at Chuck's. His jaw worked up and down, but no words escaped. All the color drained out of his face. He looked like he might pass out at any moment. Suddenly, he seemed to regain his composure, turned around, and ran from the house, his screams echoing his passage.

The shadow figure cackled loudly. The sound turned my blood to ice. I heard the van starting outside; its tires squealing as it sped down the street. I was alone in the house with the shadow thing again.

"Please… please, don't kill me," I said. "I'll let you have the house. I'll leave. Just leave me alone!"

"Leave me alone," The shadow's voice grated.

It rushed from the other room and stood in front of me. An amorphous dark figure, like a liquid darkness, coalesced before my eyes.

"Get out. Leave now!"

I sprinted from the house, jumped into my sports car and peeled out of the driveway backwards. I mashed the accelerator to the floor, roaring away as fast as I could drive.

*

I never returned.

After Eric fled the house he gibbered incessantly about what happened with the shadow entity. Naturally, no one believed him. He became so mentally unbalanced from that night that he remains a permanent resident in the county psychiatric hospital.

I tried to sell the house. Rumors of those terrible events prevented it. Two people dead; a third driven insane.

The bank eventually foreclosed on the property. Someone bought the house several months later. The new owners demolished that house of horror, building a new house in its place. They hoped it was enough to rid it of the stigma of death and insanity that clung to every room… the shadow man's legacy.

Meanwhile, I moved into a new house in another city, as far from my old haunted one as I could get.

One night, several weeks after settling in, I was getting ready for bed one night. I turned all the lights out. I lay my head on the pillow, I was almost asleep.

"I'm here for you now, Derek," the voice rasped next to my face.

L'UOMO NERO

by

Richard Groller

The Papal States, 1813

This time, the head and entrails of the murdered child were hung from the gates of the Cathedral of St. Venantius. It was not only an affront to man, but a brazen affront to God. The poor acolyte who discovered the abomination screamed, then wept uncontrollably. For the seventh time in seven months, a horror was visited upon Comune di Fabriano, an inland village of the March of Ancona, in the heart of the Apennine Mountains. The darkness that haunted Fabriano in the densely forested shadow of Monte Maggio had grown to a new level of malignancy.

When I heard the screams, I ran from the rectory to the gate of the minor basilica. I immediately vomited from the stench of the splayed gore. Then I crossed myself and blessed the remains. Others began to gather around the inconsolable acolyte, the din of their cries an affront to senses already raw. I knew of the other incidents, each more heinous than the last, but they had not been of immediate concern to me – until now. I knew with certain urgency what I needed to do – but I must first find my brother Giacomo.

*

I am only a priest. My name is Father Marco Sforza, and I have lived in Fabriano all my life. My brother Giacomo is more worldly – a former *condottiere*, now a town policeman or *sbirri*, he is a bit of a bastard and enforces order quite vigorously. Though this was not a military occupation, he was billeted, as is the custom here, in the private home of the Fiorenza family. The family had their seven year old daughter taken on the full moon. It was her head on the gate.

My brother had organized the night watch two months after the abductions began, and had been brutal in his interrogations of likely suspects and suspicious travelers. The first child's head and intestines were found outside of the village on the wooded roadside leading to Monte Maggio, and attributed to careless parents and wild animals. The second head was found hanging from a cross on a roadside shrine on the road to the Grotte di Frasassi. The intestines were hung like a shroud on the arms of the cross. That awoke the authorities from their complacency.

The townsfolk were agitated and afraid, speaking of the Diavoletti or the Babau or *l'uomo nero* come to steal the *bambinos*. Attendance at Mass was up. Families became even more insular and untrusting, and business was down at the inns and shops. My brother, less superstitious and more understanding of the dark nature of man, was more inclined to believe it was a Masonic anarchist trying to undermine Papal authority, or worse, the *living* embodiment of *l'uomo nero* – the Boogey Man – a lunatic who strikes on the full moon, described to disobedient children in bedtime stories as a tall man in a heavy black coat, with a black hood that hides his face, who punishes naughty children.

The mountainous nature of the March region allows little travel north and south, except by rough roads over the passes. The watch was made up of volunteers who guarded the roads into Fabriano. Their efforts were futile. The abducted children were now to be found *in town*.

After six months, nerves were wearing thin, but the locals had not asked for outside help, the region still recovering from the aftermath of the fall of Napoleon and local wars of expansion between the Great Houses of Savoy, Bourbon and Hapsburg.

I arrived at the Fiorenza home to find Giacomo and Signore Fiorenza out searching for the child. They had not slept since the child had been taken. I broke the bad news to Signora Fiorenza myself, and offered her what scant comfort the words of a priest could provide to a mother who had lost a young child.

Meanwhile, while I was at the Fiorenza home, Giacomo and Signore Fiorenza had arrived at the Cathedral. When I arrived back at the rectory, another priest filled me in on what had transpired. The scene was bedlam as the two men went into hysterics, and the crowd that had gathered could not calm them down. Giacomo blamed publicly himself for this particular child being a target, since he is a local symbol of constabulary authority. The crowd obliged this delusion and cajoled him for his incompetence at catching the beast who had done this. A couple of other *sbirri* arrived to disperse the crowd, and noticing his state, pulled him aside and gave him a bottle of brandy to calm his nerves. In his self-pity he ran off sobbing.

I found Giacomo about two hours before dawn, unconscious from drowning his sorrows in an aged bottle of the local Montepulciano grape. As strong as he was, his pride was dashed and he felt helpless, a fool of a constable making no progress in the chase for a living ghost. He despaired of catching this *l'uomo nero* and went to commit suicide by hanging himself, but was too drunk and failed in the attempt, having tied himself up to a tree limb, dangling with his head and limbs entwined so that his neck could not be snapped. I cut him down and took him to the rectory.

*

Next morning when he awoke, Giacomo's head was pounding and his mood was grim. "Little brother," he said to me "you should have let me die out there – I am no good to anyone anymore."

"Ah, but our beloved mother, rest her soul, would never have forgiven me for allowing you to die with your business unfinished," I replied, "and believe it or not, I have a plan for your salvation, and the salvation of the children of Fabriano."

"Don't play games with me, I am in no mood to be saved," Giacomo bellowed. "I merely want to pay for my failure to protect the people of this commune."

I shook my head gravely and said, "Your task is not complete, but I can help you in a way you cannot yet imagine. Come let me fix you some caffé and breakfast, and then we will talk."

*

After breakfast, I took my brother to the private reading room in the rectory where we would be undisturbed. I then told him a story I had never revealed to a living soul before. One summer as a young priest I had shown great promise as a scholar, and the Monsignor chose me to go to Rome for several weeks to do some research in the Vatican Library.

One day while I was there, there was much unrest in the streets. French troops had invaded the city of Rome under one of Napoleon's generals. A mob had spilled into the building to avoid being dispersed. Using the turmoil as a cover, a cutpurse had entered the Vatican Library and ran down the corridor that leads to the Vatican Archive. I saw the man knock down a Franciscan Friar carrying a sack, grab the sack, and bolt down a side passageway that led to an atrium. I took off after him and saw him vault through an open window.

I was young, fast, and naïve. I followed him across gardens and then out into the city of Rome. I chased him down alleys and over fences. I noticed the sack snag on a fence and a small wrapped package fell out of it. I snatched it up, putting it into my shirt, and continued my chase, until I rounded a corner into another alley, where three thugs grabbed me and beat me senseless. I was kicked and bludgeoned unconscious, and they stole my purse and ring. But, they managed to miss the package.

I was found, half dead, and taken to the local hospital. I was feverish and incoherent for weeks. The nuns took very good care of me, but I was unaware of their efforts. When I did not show up at the Library to continue my research, the curator asked some of the local Franciscan friars to search for me. The nuns meanwhile had sent word to the authorities and local churches that a young priest had been severely beaten. Once I was found, word was sent to the Monsignor, who came for me with a wagon and took me home to Fabriano. You were off fighting the Napoleonic scourge somewhere as a mercenary captain, so Mother nursed me back to health. Needless to say, that was the last time I went to Rome or did research for the Monsignor. The Franciscan who found me put the package in with my clothes back at my room near the Library.

Only once I was home and healthy did I realize that the package from the Vatican Library had remained with me. I opened it gingerly and with trepidation – my first thought was that I could be accused of stealing it! It was a leather bound volume, handwritten in calligraphy. It tells a story of Vatican secrets and ways to fight the forces of darkness. And I have it here.

I then went to the bottom of one of the bookcases on an interior wall in the reading room and removed a handful of books, and a false panel. Behind it was a hidden crawlspace. In it was the mysterious tome. I looked at my brother and said, "Take your time, this will be a most enlightening read," and handed him the leather volume, with a section marked for him to read.

It began, "Chronicles of the Archons: Father Valerius von Geist, Biographical Summary, Brother Nicodemus Kallinikos, S.J., Historian, October 12, 1797…" The history it told was of a vampire priest in the service of the Vatican.

*

When Giacomo was done reading, he let out a long whistle and with a half-smile said, "And you mean for us to find this *Vampiro* to solve our problems?"

"That is exactly what I mean for us to do. The journal entry is only 16 years old. If we go to Rome, we can hopefully find either Father Geist directly or perhaps Brother Kallinikos who may be able to tell us where he now resides. It is a hope that can be fulfilled and our need is dire. The Church will help us in this fight even if the temporal authorities of the Papal States cannot."

Giacomo stood and said, "Then let us waste no time. If this fairy tale is true, then by all that is Holy we must not allow another child to suffer."

*

Giacomo rode the horses hard, so it took us only two days instead of three to reach Rome. We split up – Giacomo to find lodging, and I to return to the Vatican Library. To my surprise, I discovered that Gaetano Marini was still the Prefect of the Vatican Secret Archives, all these years later. I introduced myself, and asked if he remembered the thefts in 1798 when the French annexed Rome. He gave me a pained look, saying there were so many volumes lost during the two years of the French Directory's Roman Republic, and that they did not know how many had been lost. I related my tale of innocence and pain, and he brightened, for he remembered hearing about what had happened to me. He brightened even more when I said that I had gift for the Archive that I had been safekeeping all these years. But, when I handed him the Journal, his eyes darkened.

In hushed tones, he queried, "And, you have read this?"

I admitted, "Yes, that is the reason I am here. I need to speak to Father Geist."

His stare bored right through me – "You, you do not know what you ask."

So I pleaded, telling him the tale of Fabriano and *l'uomo nero* and begging, "If he cannot help, I have nowhere else to go."

Marini got very quiet, and when he finally spoke, it was in a whisper, "Come back tomorrow evening. I cannot promise you success, but I will speak to the appropriate authorities on your behalf."

*

That evening the brothers Sforza were met by the brothers Marini at the entrance to the Vatican Archive. The Vatican Archives actually had two Prefects – the brothers Gaetano and Cosimo Marini. They were ushered in and brought to a small reading room off the main corridor. It was there they met a tall pale priest, simply dressed, but imposing in demeanor. Cosimo introduced him simply as, "Father Valerius." After the introductions, Father Valerius got right to the point, "Tell me about your Diavoletti."

Giacomo, being more intimate with details of the investigation, took the lead in this discussion. He spared no detail, relating the gruesome facts surrounding the murders of seven innocent children. The Archon took it all in, and finally asked, "So you have exhausted all options that the State can muster?"

Giacomo replied, "Fabriano's voice is small, and Ancona is poor after the wars. The authorities do not view the lives of a few mountain children as significant enough to warrant an effort. We are on our own."

Father Valerius replied, "Then I will help you. I must make some arrangements. I will meet you at St. Venantius four nights hence. Until then, go with God."

*

The brothers Sforza thanked the Prefects for their efforts and trust, and returned to the inn to get some sleep before the trip back home.

Giacomo observed, "*Il Vampiro* looks pretty good for one over a century and a half old. Do you really believe it is the will of God that we seek help from the Undying?"

My response was hesitant, but truthful, and solemn, "I believe that God works in mysterious ways that we mere mortals were never meant to understand. The knowledge of this arcana brought to light is what disturbs me. I always felt that my brush with death and my serendipitous discovery of these secrets had a purpose. I believe that purpose is now unfolding. My only wish is that we prevent any more murders, even if, we cannot tell the tale. *Ex tenebris in lucem, sic rursus in tenebras.* "

Giacomo felt a chill down his spine, "Yes. From Darkness into the Light, and back again into the Darkness. Let us hope that at the least, we will live."

*

Upon arriving at St. Venantius, we were met by a Franciscan and a Jesuit, who were an advance party of Archons, and we were ushered to the private quarters of Bishop Umberto Falconetti, the senior prelate of the Cathedral of St. Venantius. The Archons, Brother Benedetto Nuciforo and Father Enrico Scalzi, were "locals," in the sense they were attached to the Office of the Papal Legate for the March of Ancona. Bishop Falconetti was visibly discomfited by the unannounced visit, and the unwelcome attention it brought to his generally quiet and rustic surrounds. The Archons made it clear they were of the opinion this was a local police matter and were curious as to how it rose to the level of the regional Governor's office of the Papal States. The Bishop, unaware of the impetuous actions of one of his priests, was at a loss to explain this escalation of a local matter to such high profile.

As I cleared my throat to confess to my part in bringing this matter to the attention of the Vatican, a figure emerged from a shadowed corner of the room as if out of nowhere. It was Father Valerius. "Your Excellency, the Holy Father asks after your continued good health," he paused for effect and continued, "and the matter of the activities of the secret society of the Carbonari in the lands under your care." The Bishop's face blanched white and he began to shake. My brother's eyebrows rose in comprehension of the nuance and gravity of the vampire's remark.

Unbeknownst to me, the Carbonari, a secret society that sought to overthrow the absolute monarchies of Europe and the Papacy, was active in the Marches and trying to undermine the authority of the Papal States. They did not hesitate to accomplish their ends by assassination and armed revolt. Cardinal Consalvi and Cardinal Pacca would soon issue an edict against secret societies, in particular against Freemasonry and the Carbonari. The edict would forbid Catholics – under penalty of excommunication – to become members of these secret associations. The Carbonari included in their members people from all classes, to include government officials of high rank, military officers, and even members of the clergy.

Father Valerius locked his gaze with the Bishop. After a few moments, the Bishop stopped shaking. After a few questions, the Bishop calmly and quietly began to list the names of the anarchists that were subverting the authority of the Papacy in the Marches. We were the official witnesses to this interrogation/confession. The Bishop was held incommunicado and put under house arrest. Now, it was only a matter of purging the list.

My brother and I assisted Father Valerius and the Archons in assigning an order to the list of probable suspects. Of the twenty names, the list was broken into the street thugs (common criminals and muscle), the malcontents (merchants, low level officials), and those with the intellect to organize a conspiracy. The malcontents and the organizers were put on a watch list for surveillance. Over the next week, a dozen thugs were brought in for questioning. Each of them were subjected to the same questioning technique. Those with active crimes that "confessed" would endure the tender mercies of Giovanni Battista Bugatti, the executioner of the Papal States. During the two years of the French Directory, the guillotine was introduced, and it was getting a fair bit of usage.

One thug in particular, a butcher named Mario Conti, was extremely hostile and resisted arrest forcefully, to the point of injury and an on-foot chase through the town. Brother Benedetto suffered a stab wound, but Conti was finally subdued. That evening, during the interrogation, *l'uomo nero* was revealed. We all listened in disgust and horror. He had been found guilty by a secret court of the Roman Inquisition as a heretic. He was imprisoned and tortured. The Napoleonic Wars broke out. His family was made destitute, and his wife and six children all became sick during an outbreak of typhus and died. He vowed revenge against the Church for the death of his family. He bided his time and became an eager soldier of the Carbonari, willing to do whatever he was asked to do to further the cause. His campaign of terror was unilateral and unsanctioned, a private war of atrocity against the innocents of the Church, that was his doing alone, emboldened by the protection the Bishop had afforded to his cell of conspirators.

When Father Valerius was done extracting the confession, he was righteously angry. His visage contorted, and as he woke the Boogey Man from his trance, he grabbed him by the throat and, lifting him up off his feet with one hand, snarled, "Behold the Wrath of God!" His fangs sprang forward, and we were all taken aback by the ferocity of what we were witnessing. But it was not to be. *L'uomo nero's* eyes went wide, then he convulsed and slumped in the vampire's grip. A massive heart attack – he had been scared to death.

*

The Church, of course, kept the entire affair quiet. My brother was promoted and founded a pre-cursor of the Pontifical Volunteers, an armed militia drawn from the most conservative Catholics and used as a paramilitary auxiliary to the regular police. The Archons on occasion would conduct special tribunals to try suspected rebels outside of the regular court system. Giacomo maintained the surveillance network, and in 1817, when a major revolt occurred led by the Carbonari against the Marches, it was successfully put down.

With the death of the Bishop, I became the Monsignor of St Venantius. It was reported that the Bishop took ill and died of anemic blood loss while under house arrest, but that story was not completely true. The Papal Legate made a present of the Bishop to Father Valerius "to do as he willed," for his betrayal of the Church and his complicity with the Diavoletti. So Father Valerius obliged the Papal Legate and insured justice was carried out.

He ate him.

BAD MUSTARD

by

Bill Snider

"I have to know; it is something that I have to do."
*"Mustard, no; you don't have to do it. You can stay
    here with us. This is madness!"*
"I'm sorry, but I must. I have to know if I can fly."
"But, you can't! It is suicide!"
"I'm going to fly! Wheeeeeeee…"
Splat.

"Clean up on aisle five, Jimmy!" blared over the store's loud-speakers. Jimmy resented it; they always sent him to do the shit work. He sighed and went to look for the mop and bucket. No doubt some dill hole dropped a bottle of something messy and it was going to stink. He hated aisle five. That's where all the condiments were kept. Mustard and ketchup and relish and other stuff – blah.

He knew that unlike most of his friends, family and neighbors he was special: he could never stand any of that crap on his food. The smell alone would drive him nuts.

Jimmy moved out, the bucket's wheels clackity-clacking along as he pushed it with the mop in the can. The night could not pass quickly enough – he just wanted it to be over with so that he could go home and flop into bed and pass out. The whole week, for what it was worth, could just drop-kick itself into oblivion, and he'd be happy. A small town mom and pop grocery store was the last place he wanted to work, but it was the only thing he could pick up in this town. Dreams of a future, an education, and a life away in a big city surfaced and floated around his mind as he made it to aisle five.

As he expected, it was another bottle of mustard that lay smashed and splattered across the floor. The odor was pungent, wafting upward.

"Seriously, what is wrong with people? It's like they come in here and they think they're in a barn, or some such," Jimmy mumbled; he found that since he started work here in the summer, he had begun to mumble things to himself more. If he ever got into that Psych course that he wanted to take, he'd probably want to examine his reasons for doing so, but, instead, he went back into the back room to fetch a dustpan and broom.

It was short work to sweep up the pieces of glass and most of the yellowish grey vegetable matter. Mopping up the remains took a little bit longer, and made a disgusting mash of water and mustard. Jimmy could not look into the bucket for long without thinking about vomiting; that was how bad he felt about the stuff.

"Hey, Jimmy; Aisle Five Syndrome?" The voice startled him, approaching from behind and without warning.

"What? Oh, hey, Sally; sorry, lost in thought. Didn't hear ya coming by. Syndrome? What do ya mean?"

Now that she was there and talking with him, he couldn't help but notice Sally – pert and perky as the other workers liked to describe her. There were other, less flattering things said, but he never listened when Ryan or Cory spoke – they were Neanderthals with no sense of class.

She was cute and probably one of the more considerate of his fellow workers at the Corner Shoppe Grocer where they worked. Long brown hair, hazel eyes, and tight jeans; *that*, was Sally. Always smelling like some kind of exotic flower, she was cheery and polite and not the least bit condescending – at least not that he'd ever noticed.

"Yeah; Aisle Five Syndrome. Stuff is always breaking here. Marge and Leroy think it's somebody working here that keeps doing it, but nobody is ever around when something breaks." She had a voice that reminded Jimmy of a singer's – even and melodic.

"Tell me about it; they keep sending me over here to clean the shi– … stuff up. I know they own the place and all, but it's not like it's my fault this stuff gets smashed." He put the last swish of the mop back into the bucket, the mess now eradicated and the floor looking spotless, if a little shiny from the water.

"Well, have fun, Sunshine; I gotta get back to cash. I'm sure the late evening rush will be starting soon."

Sally moved on past him to the front of the store. Jimmy watched as she sashayed past, a hint of lilac in the air as she disappeared. He sighed, as he pushed the bucket back to the storeroom. Pushing the whole mess to dock C, he paused long enough to open the loading dock door. The garbage bin was located here. It was not the proper way to dispose of the mess – he didn't care; he was tired and just wanted to go home. Besides, it wasn't like anybody was going to either care or be put out by it. He dumped the bucket into the garbage bin, the broken glass and the soiled water mixing in the disgusting mess that was already in the trash. It all settled to the bottom.

He closed the door and went back to work.

"Oh, Relish; why did he have to do that?" Ketchup cried plain-tively.

"I really can't say for sure, my dear; that boy was a troubled soul. Always touching the dark, always talking up a torrent of pain and suffering."

"But, it was certainly a suicide thing to do, wasn't it?"

"Absolutely; but, that lad had issues that we can't even hope to understand."

"Relish, it just makes me so sad. I thought I was getting to finally understand him, and now he's gone."

"I know... I know."

*

"So, Sally mentioned something about Aisle Five Syndrome. Is this seriously something we're calling it?" Jimmy addressed his friend, George, the only other summer addition to the Grocer. George was the quiet, dark, almost-Goth-devoted, but not quite the black-fingernails–and-eye-makeup type. It was one of his contentions that for every cheerleader or jock, there was a Goth or an almost-Goth lurking near-by.

"Heh; you and Sally hunh, Psych boy? Good for you," George made the last part sound sarcastic without even putting much edge on his tone.

"First, piss off; you make that sound dirty and you're not even Cory, that fucktard. Second, stick to the topic. Aisle Five, what's up with that?" They were in aisle five, and nobody else was about, so Jimmy felt safe talking about the others that worked there; but he still kept his voice down. He looked at the clock on the far wall and saw they still had another seven minutes before their break ended, which would be their last break before their shift finished.

Jimmy looked at his friend, patiently waiting for an answer. They'd known each other for the last five years, having finished high school together and deciding to make a break for higher learning as a team. They were still trying to scrape together enough for tuition to match what their folks were willing to contribute. Another year, may-be, saving and scraping together and they'd be able to leave this town for larger horizons.

"Yeah, sure, Cory and Ryan started calling it that after they heard Sally use it casually the one time. I think they were trying to be insult-ing, but it's now beginning to stick," George pushed the hair out of his eyes and regarded his friend with an admonishing glance. He continued, "look, I was doing some research last night, about this place. There is some seriously messed up shit on the history of this piece of land."

"What? You actually used the computer for something other than porn? Who are you and what have you done with my friend, George?"

"Oh, and ain't you the little f-tard, you and your girlfriend, Sally," George crossed his arms, and glared at Jimmy.

"Fine, go on; I assume there was a point somewhere in your history lesson?" Jimmy waved his friend on, bowing slightly to add to the friendly condescension.

"Right, so get this: apparently, about thirty years ago, this whole area was forest, completely covered with trees and bushes and shit. The town was even way smaller than we think it is now, maybe two hundred souls all counted. They were working on roads here, connecting one main road to the other way up north or something. That's Main Street, now, by the way – the street out front. Their work laid the foundation for our main thoroughfare of today. We wouldn't be working here, the whole main street wouldn't be here if it wasn't for that.

"So, this guy, Darvin Maynin, apparently went psycho; he worked on the road crew that was building this little crisscross network of road along with a bunch of other guys. He went nuts around this time, and started to surreptitiously kill a bunch of people as the crew moved north. He'd pick people at random, when they weren't suspecting it and just haul ass on them. No rhyme, no reason on who or how.

"He used a shovel a lot, a pickaxe a few times, a hammer once or twice. Messy little prick, he was. And it was always in the woods, away from the roadwork. According to the news clips, he got away with it for a long time, because nobody noticed who was missing. It wasn't until a local couple – one Adam and Marie something-or-other – disappeared that the cops got anything to go on.

"It turns out, this is where he liked to bury the bodies – right around here, where the Grocer was later built. It was here, where they found the bodies of the couple, and the cops nailed his ass right over the spot where they dug the bodies up afterwards. As the news story goes, he didn't want to cooperate nicely when they found him. So, in the takedown, they were forced to shoot him dead.

"So, I *think*... the Grocer is haunted. Is all I'm saying," George nodded his head vigorously, as if that was enough proof to back up his claim.

"Haha! Seriously?"

Both young men turned, startled by the peal of laughter from Sally. They had not heard her walk up the aisle.

"Uh, yeah, uh, right, haunted. It's what the Internet says," George replied, self-conscious and unsure of himself.

"Well, I guess it's possible, if one accepts that sort of thing," Jimmy piped up, defending his friend, even though he wasn't quite one with the same opinion.

"Okay, Jimmy! It works for the movies, but this is the Town of Ignace; we don't have excitement here. I believe your break is up now anyway; you boys better get back to the stock room. I heard Marge asking about when the condiment section was going to get faced up," She crossed past them toward the break room.

"Okay, thanks, Sally!" Jimmy replied as he hastily got up and left.

"I still say it's haunted," George threw it over his shoulder, more as a taunt.

"Okay, Goth-boy; whatever floats your freaky little boat," Sally smiled to take the sting out as she kept going toward her own break time.

*

"Relish, is that true, what that young man said? Are we dispossessed souls? I have a memory of trees, peaceful and pleasant, but then... something unpleasant," she cried, as unsure now as at any other time she'd ever been.

"Ketchup, it does seem to ring true somehow, but I don't know how. There must be something about it all that makes sense. According to that fellow, those events happened thirty years ago where have we been all that time? Here, just waiting? Waiting for what?" He talked calmly, sure of himself if nothing else.

"So, why are we being punished? What should we be doing?" She wanted to cry, but there was no way to do so, being a bottle of ketchup on a grocery store shelf.

"Wait and see, is all that we can do for now. If an opportunity presents itself for something to be done, then we should rise to the occasion; otherwise, we must merely bide our time," he remained calm, assertive, comforting as he stood regally upon the shelf, a relish of a simpler time.

"I don't like it; I have a bad feeling about all this."

*

"Hey, Cory; look what we got here. It's Jimmy the Joke and Goth-boy George!"

Cory just grunted, never being much of a talker. He was basically Ryan's shorter, stockier, quieter, and rough and tumble sidekick. Ryan, on the other hand, was a mean sort of man. He was brutish and unsavory, large and solid; his idea of a good time was to get drunk and go out and piss on anyone who had the audacity to come near him. He was one of those fellows who, in high school, were sure that they were going to make it in the arena of football, but somehow missed the boat. His lack of wit, however, made it less clear to him about exactly how far he had missed that boat.

Most days when he came to work, he was either hung-over or still working through the previous night's drunk. He was an unpleasant fellow to work with at the best of times, and could be mostly avoided as he worked in the back room almost exclusively. He was strong and could be relied on to unload trucks and stack boxes where they needed to be, but Marge and Leroy knew better than to let him work the floor.

"Ryan, we're looking for Marge. We were told she was looking for us," Jimmy kept his gaze down, and made sure to keep a simple tone.

"What do I look like, a fucking message board? She was back here a few minutes ago; I have no idea where she went." Ryan waved the two young men off, and turned back to pulling the skid out of the truck that he was unloading. The product looked cold, so it meant that it was going into the freezers. Nobody liked working the freezers, so it was obvious that Ryan was crankier than he normally would be.

"Uh, okay," Jimmy motioned George back toward Dock C, where they could at least get a good glance out to the back of the building. The door was often left open to allow a breeze into the back room. Marge liked to inspect the back lot to make sure that buggies weren't being left there. Those cost money.

"What do ya, think, Jimmy?" George pointed out the doorway. "All this could be yours for the low, low price of your soul!" he leered with a bantering smarmy tone and a light smile, unusual for his face. Jimmy thought it might crack. He laughed.

"George, you're a freak."

Together they stared out into the night gloom, the heavy-duty sulfur lights casting a stark weight of doom into the lot. Only the employees parked back here, as it was where the trucks came and went for deliveries and pickups.

Jimmy heard a noise in the garbage bin, and looked down. He couldn't see anything in there clearly; shadows cast wicked outlines in the deep bin amongst all the refuse that got thrown in there daily. Movement; he thought he saw movement, but wasn't sure.

"Rats," Jimmy pointed down for George's benefit.

"Ugh; come on, let's go back out front. She probably wants us to collect buggies from the front lot; it's about that time. Sally or somebody should know where she is by now."

"Sure, let's go."

*

"Ow, ow, ow! What the hell is biting me?" Mustard looked down and saw that a small trail of ants had begun to retrieve small bits of his yellowish self and move them back along their line of food retrieval.

"What the...?"

"And, hold on; I survived the fall?"

"I'm confused!"

He tested the limits of his body. Having been trapped in a glass container for what seemed like an eternity left nothing to shape an awareness of body from. He was an ungainly organic slop sitting at the bottom of a waste bin.

"Would you ants STOP EATING ME?" he shouted at the small insects, but they ignored him. They kept taking small pieces from his body and moving it back to their nest or home or whatever it was that they did with food. A pseudopod formed without him trying to concentrate on it specifically – it was more as a result of him wanting to smack the ants and stop them from consuming more of his essence.

"STOP, STOP, STOP!" he shouted as the unconsciously formed hand smashed down on their tiny bodies. They squished, the yellow mustard matter inundating their tiny lives. As he did this, he realized that these creatures, as minute as they were, were tasty. This was new, startling and compulsively distracting. With each tiny body that he consumed, he felt better, stronger, more in tune with himself. Their small organic substance quickly broke down and added to his.

Quickly, he ate all of those that had followed the pheromone trail to his body. There were no more of the insects around him, but he could tell that more were off in the direction that the earlier units had moved to – he could sense them, and the bits of himself that had gone away with them.

It took him some time to realize it, but he discovered that he could ooze himself along, and he crawled back along the way the ants had gone, following the sense of where his remaining essence was. In the process, he also came to understand, that he could shape his mustard body into a form. Unconsciously, he stood up, and assumed the form that he most remembered in a faraway life, bipedal and ambulatory. It was a rough approximation of a human form, but he felt much happier after noticing that he had done so.

He continued to walk, following the trail of ants, unceremoniously stomping them the whole way along, absorbing their organic mass into his own. Single-mindedly, he kept up the attack against the ant community that had sought to eat him. By the time he reached the ant colony, he had amassed quite a bit of ant organic material, and had grown by a perceptible fraction. Without thinking it through, he punched down into the ant hole in the pavement, oozing his form down and deep and thoroughly throughout the colony.

Everywhere that he encountered their little forms, he absorbed them, as his mustard mass quested through the colony to find every last bit of himself that had been stolen from him. Soon, he was finished, and felt complete, having added even more mass to his body as a whole. After oozing back to the body central, he stood back up, noticing that he now was almost a foot and a half tall.

He felt good, even though he still looked like mustard.

*

"Okay, so if we accept that your premise is correct, that the Grocer is haunted, what then? And why is it only starting to become an issue now-ish?" Jimmy lightly punched George's shoulder.

"Ow; I dunno. I'm not an expert on this stuff. I just read stuff and that's what I read."

George saw Sally at the front, cash ringing through a customer, and instead pulled Jimmy toward the front entrance

"So, what can happen in a haunted grocery store? So far, all we've seen is a couple of jars of mustard and stuff thrown at the floor. What next? Are we going to get sucked into a black hole like in that movie? Is there going to be a little girl getting sucked into a TV? What, what, what, I say," Jimmy was having fun ribbing his friend.

"It's getting close to closing time; we should probably go out and collect the buggies."

George looked around the store; it was pretty empty of customers at this point, being as it was about midnight. For about another hour or two, staff would continue cleaning up. But, in the meantime, it was that eerie point of the day in which a normally busy environment suddenly becomes filled with only a few souls. Sometimes, it freaked him out; sometimes he welcomed what he called the tea time dark of his day.

"Sure, okay. But, back to this haunted thing. What's the point? Why would a ghost or poltergeist or whatever want to haunt a place, or a thing, or whatever?" Jimmy continued on the discussion, curious now.

"Dunno, perhaps it wants vengeance? Or maybe just to settle a score? Maybe it just wants to finish something? Maybe it just wants to have fun? I didn't get too much time to dig into things. It's not like I know the whole back-story of those people. May not even be them; it could be some other even older or newer set of unhappy spirits. I dunno," George was getting uncomfortable now; he knew that every- one thought he was death-inclined, but the reality of it scared the crap out of him whenever he thought about it seriously.

"Vengeance, hunh?" Jimmy let it drop as they separated to collect various buggies that had been left scattered throughout the front park- ing lot.

*

Mustard felt good as he looked around. It was a mass of con- fusing stimuli. All these things with purposes and uses; his head was fuzzy-filled and he wasn't quite able to keep his thoughts clear: the words in his mind moved slowly, like deep ocean currents: turbulent, turgid, twisting through paths of sluggish stagnation; each thought drip-dropping to lie at the bottom of whatever metaphysical equivalent for a brain might exist.

But, he thought he was hungry. This was a new and unusual sensation for him. Being sealed in a jar for many years, trapped on a shelf, with no real sense of self, provided for a distinct lack of sensations. He wanted to explore what he could do, and what his limits were, yearning for the opportunity to be physical.

The garbage bin provided some choice chances to experiment. Punch. Jump. Heft. Mustard tried various actions against the refuse that layered the inside of the bin. He found that he felt no pain, except for that which he associated with pain. Even though the ants were eating bits of him, he hadn't actually felt that as pain; rather, he knew it should be associated as pain. This was deep thinking for him.

For now, though, he was hungry.

The ants were a good first go; now he wanted, needed, to find something more substantial. That's when he spied the rat, secretly scurrying through the bin at the very edges of its metal container. No, there was more than one. There were several; all of them busily searching the bin for the choicest bits of food.

Mustard waited for his opportunity; he remained quiet, poised at the edge of a box of long-gone cookies. He didn't have to wait too long – he smelled of food to the rats, so he was a natural bit of bait. The first one came right up to him, sniffing, its whiskers fluttering, scenting the air for treasure and alarm.

It crept closer to him. Without warning, he lunged with his whole body, pouring himself right down its gullet, suffocating the rat with his mustardy self almost instantly. The rat didn't even have time to squeal its last sound before it died; and from the inside to the outside, Mustard absorbed the rat's body, blood, bone, and muscle all.

Mustard then hunted down the remaining rats, slaughtering them all, just like rats in a garbage bin.

*

"Ok, everybody, listen up. Tomorrow's going to be a big day. We've got Donna and Lester from the meat packers coming by to visit. We want to have a spanking clean store to show them when they get here; so, everybody hop to it and let's get this place in shape," Marge liked pep talks; she was the queen of them, according to some. Almost like a mother hen, she would make sure that everything was in its right place, with the right amount of attention lavished on it. She treated people like that, too.

She and Leroy – who for the most part either stayed in the office or stayed away, ostensibly carrying on the outside work of negotiating with suppliers and major customers – had owned the Grocer for close to a decade now. They built the place from the ground up, with the money that they had earned in the big city, having escaped to this little slice of country heaven.

"Cory, Ryan – you boys got the back room sorted out?"

"Yes, ma'am," they both chorused.

"Good! Can you boys grab brooms then and start the sweeping?"

They nodded and moved away, back to the stockroom to grab the dry mops. The store, now closed, was empty of customers so prime cleaning time could begin.

"George, Jimmy – the counters in Aisle five faced up?" she looked around for their faces.

"Yes, ma'am," Jimmy answered, as George kept silent.

"Sally, you and the other cashiers finished your cash-outs?"

"Yes, ma'am; all locked up," Sally replied.

Marge smiled; she liked this part of the day. It was kind of like being a drill sergeant and a mom all wrapped up in one little package of fun. Leroy, he was at home, probably on the computer at this time of night; but she – she enjoyed locking up the place. He, on the other hand, preferred to open. She watched the little dance of the employee end of night close-up. A perfectly orchestrated operation where all the staff came together to hurry up and finish the last little bit of work so that they could all leave.

There was a rule at the Grocer for the end of day routine: Everyone stays and everyone goes. Nobody was allowed to leave at shift's end if somebody still had something left to do. If everything was ready to go early, then everybody got to leave early. This, or so Marge was often inclined to say, bred an attitude of collaboration and cooperation; or, at least that's what she liked to believe.

It was only twenty after twelve, and it looked like everything and everyone would be ready to go right at half-past. The cashiers milled at the front, the stock boys kept joking about and only the back room rowdies were left to be seen, still needing to finish up the final sweep.

That's when the commotion began.

Ryan hollered out a harshly-worded yell, followed quickly by a frenzied Cory running to the front of the Grocer. The sound of something being struck repeatedly could be heard clearly through the corner supermarket. Cory, in a ragged sweat, pointed back to the way he'd come and spoke as clearly as he could.

"There's something back there; something big, something ugly. And it attacked me and Ryan. Ryan tried to fight it. I ran; ah'm sorry, but that shit weren't right. It weren't human," he looked shaken, his skin an unhealthy pallor, moreso than anybody Jimmy had ever seen before.

"Cory! Talk straight, son; was it a raccoon? A bear? What was it?" Marge took the young man abruptly by the shoulders, trying to shake some sense out of him.

"No ma'am. It was about three feet tall and it was yellow, roughly man-shaped. And, it didn't growl, nor make no noise whatsoever. It was unnatural. It came from nowhere and just... it just... it... it chomped down on Ryan's arm and ate it!" Cory's eyes darted roughly around as he glanced back at the storeroom he had escaped. Some of the cashiers gasped at that; Jimmy and George shared a look.

"Jimmy, do we have any kind of weapons out front here?" Marge looked directly at him as he thought that through. He glanced back at George again and struck upon a thought. George seemed to hit the same idea at the same idea.

"Shovels!"

There were a couple in the front office.

"Well? Go git them. Hurry!"

Jimmy and George both took off at a run.

"Sally, call the Sheriff's office. Tell them to send somebody over quick."

George and Jimmy returned in minutes. The tableau remained the same: Cashiers huddled at the front, Cory almost bawling his eyes out, the other stock clerks milling, unsure of what to do, and Marge directing everybody to stay calm and work things out.

"Okay, you two, go check the back room and see what's going on."

"Us?" Jimmy and George both chimed at the same time.

"Yes – you two; you've got the shovels, don't you?"

"Oh," defeated, they headed cautiously to the back of the Grocer. The noise, what had sounded like a struggle, had died down; there was no sound coming from the back room anymore. It was deathly quiet. Jimmy motioned to George to open the door while he kept his shovel high and ready to smash down. George was ready to jab.

He pulled the door open quickly, jumping back out of the way for Jimmy to swing if need be. Nothing jumped out at them. They stood for a moment, looking inside, trying to see what was going on. It was quiet, too quiet. It looked normal, *too* normal. Then George pointed, and Jimmy saw it.

Ryan, miserable bastard that he was, lay in a pool of blood on the floor near Dock C. He wasn't moving. Hunched over his body, a fuzzy figure, almost human-shaped, was quietly gnawing on his leg. It was quiet, and moved with a minimum of effort. All of a sudden, the odor hit Jimmy. It was the dense, cloying, sickly-sweet smell of mustard. He almost wanted to throw up. That's when he remembered the bucket from earlier.

Jimmy motioned George to back up, quietly letting the door settle back into place. They huddled close, and spoke in soft tones.

"It's fucking mustard, George!"

"No shit, Jim-lock!"

"And, it was eating Ryan, the poor bastard."

"Yeah, and so, what are we gonna do next?" George looked worried as he swiped another glance at the door and through the window. He could still see the yellow form munching away.

"Water," Jimmy said so quietly, that George thought he must have missed something.

"What?"

"Water. Oh, and Olive Oil; lots of Olive Oil! Come on! Back to aisle five!"

*

"Relish, what's going on? There's a lot of commotion."

"Indeed there is. This is most surprising. It seems that Mustard is still around, and he seems to have sprouted legs. And, most gruesomely, he's handling himself well. Most interesting."

"How can you sit there and talk like that? This is horrible! My little Mustard is becoming a monster!"

"Indeed he is. And here I didn't think he had it in him…"

"What do you mean by that, Relish? What do you mean?"

"I think we'll see soon enough, my dear."

*

"I smash, you splash. Got it?"

George didn't think it would work, but it was the best plan they had, so he nodded. Otherwise, their gooses would be cooked, or at the very least eaten. Not a pleasant or pretty sight in his mind, either way.

They had grabbed a few one-gallon jugs of olive oil and lined them up by the door to the stockroom. George cracked open the seals of all six jugs, and readied two in his hands. Quietly, they opened the door, propping it open with the doorstopper at its bottom. The mustard was still hunched over Ryan, almost finished with eating his leg and ready to go for the torso.

Jimmy wanted to gag at the smell; spilled blood and mustard did not make for a pleasant scent. They took several deep breaths, and on the silent count of three, Jimmy rushed into the room, raising the shovel high overhead; George followed closely. Surprised, Mustard looked up and rolled slowly to the right, still consuming a ligament or two.

Jimmy brought down the shovel with all the strength that he could muster. It smashed resoundingly against the floor, passing right through the yellow fuzzed man-shaped thing. Mustard splattered across the floor. George, right behind Jimmy, half sprayed half poured the olive oil all across the floor, all over the mustard splatter.

Jimmy kept smashing Mustard, mixing the mustard and the olive oil turning them into a yellower, more pungent and much thinner goo.

"Get the mop! Get the mop!"

George ran over to the wall and pulled over the big dry mop. Together, Jimmy and George manhandled the mop, soaking up a lot of the oil and mustard mix. The rest of the slop they pushed to the edge of the dock and back into the garbage bin.

"Now what?" George asked.

"Fire, lots of it."

"What?"

"George, quick; go back out and get some lighter fluid and matches!" Jimmy mopped whatever leftovers still littered the floor into the bin. Some bits seemed to try and rise of their own accord, but he quickly smooshed them with the dry mop. He pushed them as hard as he could back into the bin.

George returned quickly with a couple of bottles of campfire lighter fluid. The first bottle they upended straight into the bin, where most of the goo was congealing and taking shape again. The second and third bottles they sprayed all around the bin's contents, coating them with as much fluid as possible. There were lots of boxes, skids and other trash already in there.

George handed Jimmy an old style book of matches. He struck the first match, folded back the cover, and lit the rest of them. The book fizzled brightly as the flame caught. He let the fire really take hold, then threw it into the bin. There was a soft whoosh as the lighter fluid immediately took to the flame and started burning brightly. The yellow goo at the bottom bubbled vilely, as the rest of the contents of the bin soon caught up with the lighter fluid, the fire burning strong.

Jimmy looked at George, and George stared back. They both raised their hands palm out and exchanged a high five.

"I hate mustard, but I love olive oil!"

*

"Well, you see, my dear, I've been lying to you both for quite some time. I've never forgotten who I was. It's always been quite clear. Death was, of course, quite traumatic, but apparently more traumatic for you two than for I."

"You're scaring me now, Relish. What is going on? I don't like this being in the dark."

"That's unfortunate, my dear, Marie. You and Adam were such innocent souls; your deaths were such sweet surcease."

"What?"

"As I said, Marie, I've known all along who I am. And your poor Adam there – now washing away – has shown me a possibility that I had not even considered. I believe it is now my turn to try and fly…"

"Nooooooo, you monster!"

GRANDMA

by

Wayne Borean

"Are you sure you are okay Grandma?" Charlie was concerned. His Grandmother had been a huge part of his life. She had encouraged him to follow his dream and study folklore at the University of Toronto, instead of being a doctor like his father had wanted. Then she had encouraged him to marry his childhood sweetheart, much to the family's chagrin. She had helped him hold his life together when that marriage fell apart.

Every time that Charlie needed support Grandma had always been there for him, far more than his parents, whom he hardly ever talked to now. She hardly ever talked to them, either. He often wondered how such a warm, loving woman could have given birth to such a cold, arrogant, son-of-a-bitch like his father.

These days Grandma looked more and more frail. Her insistence on still living in the century farm house where she had lived most of her life was a concern as well. What if she fell? He thought again about broaching the idea of a cell phone that she could carry in her pocket.

He looked at her across the battered surface of the old kitchen table, that she kept near the wood burning stove in winter. That meant today it was uncomfortably warm for Charlie, but he didn't mind. It made Grandma comfortable, and that was what mattered.

He knew that she wouldn't take his suggestion. She didn't do technology. Her radio was over twenty years old, as was her color television. She refused to replace either; after all, they still worked!

Grandma sighed, "I'm old Charlie. I've been old for a long time. Don't you worry. Just bring the children by on Saturday, and I'll make some cookies, okay?"

Charlie looked at her. She smiled back at him.

"Okay Grandma. We'll be here about 10 o'clock on Saturday. All right?"

She chuckled, "That's my boy. I'll have a surprise for you and the children, so don't be late!"

*

On Saturday morning the kids were excited. Besides Charlie's two children, Crystal who was eight, from his first short marriage, and Jimmie, who was six, from his second even shorter marriage; there were the two cousins Jessica who was nine, and Luba, the adorably cute little platinum blonde who was four. Jimmie's friend Ranjit from school, and Rover, Charlie's Labrador Retriever rounded out the expedition. They all piled into Charlie's minivan for the drive to Grandma's farm.

Saturday trips to Grandma's house (well, technically Great-Grandma to them, but she didn't care what they called her, and she spoiled them rotten with love) had been a family fixture since Crystal was little. Charlie's first wife had loved Grandma at first. He never did understand why the two women came to dislike each other, and probably never would. He had tried to talk to Janet about it at one point, and had never gotten a straight answer from her. Then Janet had suddenly moved to Vancouver, and even though they were supposed to share custody he'd never heard from her again.

As he drove, he thought about his even shorter second marriage. That had been weird. One morning he woke up, and Sarah had been gone. Her purse was sitting on her night table, her car was in the drive-way, but she was nowhere to be found. He'd called the police. And then wished he hadn't. The police decided that he was the most likely suspect, and practically pulled out the rubber hose and brass knuckles. Luckily a friend of his was a criminal lawyer and decided to hang around. Steven had stepped in and protected him in ways that he didn't understand at the time.

The police never did find Sarah. Luckily they must have come to the conclusion that he wasn't involved at some point, because about a year after she disappeared they stopped bothering him. He still didn't know what happened, and probably never would.

They dropped in for a snack at the donut shop. The kids went for the usual heavily sugared stuff. Charlie settled for a Blueberry muffin, and sat back watching the kids go through their donuts like sharks, while Rover waited patiently in the van. They left, an extra muffin for Rover in Charlie's hand.

Then they swung by the grocery store to buy a week's worth of groceries for Grandma. Charlie also picked up some extra treats for Rover. Grandma always loved spoiling the dog, and Rover was her devoted buddy.

Back in the minivan they sang songs, much to Rover's annoy-ance. Rover howled when young voices hit the high notes. Charlie laughed, drawing an annoyed look from the dog. Rover put his head down on the floor of the minivan, and buried his ears under his paws as the kids insisted on singing Tom Smiths "Operation Desert Storm" over and over again.

An hour after they left the house they pulled into Grandma's driveway. Charlie felt relief at seeing the smoke drifting up from the chimney on the old house. That meant that Grandma was okay. He saw her wave from the kitchen window as he got out of the van. It took a couple of minutes to get the kids' seat belts unbuckled, grab Rover's leash and the groceries. He led the mob up to the house.

Inside Grandma's house the children chattered, telling Grandma about their week. Charlie was glad to see that Grandma didn't look any worse. She didn't look any better either, but as she said, she was getting old.

She chatted with the children while feeding them fresh oatmeal chocolate chip cookies, and milk.

Rover, after getting a treat, wandered out of the kitchen into the living room, picked a spot on the old couch, curled up, and went to sleep.

Charlie listened to Grandma and the kids as he put the groceries away. She sounded tired today. But she'd been sounding tired for the last couple of years. She really sounded happy though. She was enjoying having the kids here; he could tell that, and they were enjoying seeing her.

Once the children finished their cookies they went to the living room and turned on the television. Charlie sat down across from Grandma by the open living room door.

"How are you feeling Grandma?" He saw a smile on her face.

"Charlie, oh Charlie. You've been such a wonderful, loyal boy," she reached over to touch his check, there was a sharp pain, and then Charlie fell out of his chair, hitting his head on the table, sprawling on the floor. Grandma stood above him.

"Thank you Charlie. Thank you very much." Charlie looked up into her eyes, and saw a bronze sparkle. He fought to move, but couldn't. His muscles were like Jello. He tried to yell. Nothing came out. His mouth was open, but he couldn't make a noise. He could barely breathe.

Grandma came around the table, and knelt down beside him.

"I'm sorry, Charlie. I really am. You've been such a good boy. And I do love you, as I've never loved anyone before. But this is necessary if I am to live. Wait here. Not that you have much choice," she smiled at him. He saw a bronze glow in the back of her brown eyes.

Grandma moved away, slowly, toward the living room door, "Crystal, could you come to the kitchen please?"

Charlie lay on the floor in a daze. He heard her beautiful little voice cry out, "Yes Grandma, I'll be right there!"

A moment later her body collapsed across Charlie's legs. He struggled to move, but couldn't. He couldn't see Crystal's eyes, couldn't see her face, couldn't see her ribs to tell if she was still breathing. Grandma moved to where she could see Charlie's face and winked at him. Charlie shuddered. What was happening?

Grandma called a second time, "Jessica, could you come into the kitchen please?"

Charlie heard Jessica's feet tripping toward the kitchen door. A moment later she, too, collapsed across his lower body. Again he couldn't see her face, he couldn't tell if she was breathing. Charlie was starting to panic. He still couldn't move. Grandma once more moved to where she could look at him. Grandma looked strange. She smiled at him again. He noticed that her cheeks appeared rosier and plumper. And her hair. The white and grey was changing, darkening. Was that Grandma?

"Luba, could you come here please?" Grandma's voice sounded stronger. A moment later skipping steps approached the kitchen door, and another body collapsed across Charlie. Charlie realized he was crying. He didn't even know why. He didn't understand what was going on. Grandma again came to where he could see her, and looked at him. She smiled widely at him, bronze eyes glowing brightly.

"Jimmie, could you and Ranjit come into the kitchen please?" The voice sounded even stronger to Charlie. It also sounded triumphant. Mocking. The kids didn't notice. He heard them coming to the kitchen talking about a cartoon, and a moment later they were spread across his legs too.

"Charlie, Charlie. I've been waiting a long time for this," Grandma knelt in front of him again, hair now a rich auburn, skin now tight across high cheekbones, wonderful glowing bronze eyes staring at him. If it wasn't for the old style granny dress, and the long hair still drawn up in a bun, he wouldn't have known it was the same woman. What he saw in front of him seemed to be a small breasted girl, no more than fourteen years old.

"When my kind get old we lose our appetite. We eat hardly anything for years, until it is time to be reborn, like a phoenix," she sighed. "I was selfish when I urged you to become interested in folklore. Oh, you already were interested, thanks to Marvel Comics. I wanted to know if any more of my race existed. You never did find any. I'm not sure what I would have done if you had found them."

"But now I need to finish things."

She got up and left the kitchen, leaving Charlie helpless on the floor. She came back a minute later with the good winter coat and a track suit that Charlie had bought Grandma a couple of years before.

She knelt in front of Charlie, with the large cleaver from the kitchen counter. She laid it on the floor, and undressed herself. Once nude, she stood and spun in place in front of him.

"Nice body, isn't it?"

She felt between her legs, and shuddered with pleasure, "I'm not human, I guess, though I did bear your father to term. So maybe I am. I don't know how old I am, I can't even remember how many times I've done this. I don't even know why I'm telling you this, other than I do feel guilty because, while I never did love your father, I did love you. But I made a mistake. I let it go too long, and I needed too much energy to get young again. One body wouldn't do. It took all of you."

She paused for a moment, "It really is sad. I should have arranged something else twenty years ago, and become your wife. If I'd have known what was going to happen to your marriages I would have done that, and taken your father instead. The world would have been a better place with him gone, and you'd have been a lot happier with me as your wife. But we all make mistakes."

"Remember how I used to watch the crime shows on television? I'll drag all your bodies into the front room, and then I'll wash myself clean. Since this is my house, my fingerprints are everywhere. Then I'll dress myself in the clean clothes in the kitchen, and leave." She giggled, "I think that most crime scene investigators won't look at this as their solution!"

"Charlie, Charlie. I've been waiting a long time for this."

The newer, younger, Grandma smiled, "Maybe I'll kill your father anyway. I'm always hungry after a change. And I know he likes young girls." She giggled.

The cleaver rose, and fell with a thunk. She held up Ranjit's head. "Such energy," She kissed the forehead, then tossed the head aside. The cleaver rose and fell again. This time she held up Luba's blood-stained platinum blonde head, kissed the forehead, said, "I really did love you dear," and tossed the head aside. Then it was Crystal, then Jessica, and then Jimmie.

Grandma held up the cleaver, and licked the blade, "Goodbye Charlie." She brought the cleaver down on his neck.

Only one thing left to do. Naked, she slipped into the living room where Rover snored on the couch sleeping, placed her hands around Rover's neck, and twisted. Hard. There was a loud crack. Rover stopped breathing, fouled the couch as his bowels let loose, and changed shape so that he now looked exactly like Grandma had.

The creature that stood in the room looked about, satisfied. Young again for the first time in three hundred years. Lots of humans to prey upon. The start of a new cycle. How wonderful!

BREAKING UP IS HARD TO DO

by

John Manning

Mark Edwards stared unseeing at the computer screen. His email inbox displayed several messages, most of them unopened. He didn't need to read them to know what they said. All were filled with sympathy for his loss. Words that were meant to comfort him, like the ones in the dog-eared Bible lying open on his desk, but nothing that he cared to see.

Not tonight.

Although the monitor glowed brightly before him, all he saw was Joanna's face as he told her it was over – that final, horrible scene with her begging for one more chance as he stood cold and aloof denying every plea, every tearful entreaty. Over and over it played – an accusatory film clip. And, each replay deepened his guilt.

I shouldn't have done it. If I hadn't broken up with her, maybe none of this would have happened.

Against his will, Mark's hand moved the mouse across the pad. On the screen the cursor scrolled down until it reached an email he'd read before – read too many times before. Dorothy Fletcher. Joanna's mother. He hesitated, and then clicked the button. Immediately the screen filled with the message that had sent his world crashing around him.

Mark. I hate to be the bearer of such terrible news. David and I are still having trouble dealing with it ourselves. I know that you and Joanna are no longer together although we (Joanna, David, and me) hoped that the two of you would reconcile. This morning Joanna was found dead in that little sports car she loved.

The police believe, although it's still being investigated, that she was attacked in the parking lot as she was headed for her car. She was brutally beaten. She suffered numerous head injuries and what they called defensive injuries to her arms and hands. Evidently she fought her attacker but was not strong enough to get away. The body won't be released to us until the coroner finishes his investigation. Once that happens, we will have her cremated and her ashes scattered. There will be no memorial service. I am so sorry that you have to find out this way. Perhaps if you two had worked things out, this wouldn't have happened. We don't blame you for her death. Please don't think that.

We just wish things had been different. Dorothy.

The image blurred as tears filled his eyes. Of course she blamed him. How could she not, when he blamed himself? Wasn't he the one who did the breaking up? Didn't he decide to end the life they'd shared for the past nine years? Hadn't he pushed – no *shoved* – the first domino that ended in this horrible design?

He closed the email and picked up a tumbler of whiskey and ice from where it sat next to the keyboard. The cubes rattled discordantly against the glass. As he raised the drink to his lips, he glanced at the tiny numbers in the bottom corner of the screen Midnight. The witching hour. As he swallowed, a new message appeared above the list of unopened emails. He glanced at the sender's name. The whiskey caught in the back of his throat. His cough sprayed the keyboard and screen with amber droplets.

JoannaFletcher227. The subject line read simply: Help.

It was her user name. Almost. The 227 was wrong. She used 35 after her name. It had to be a joke. Someone was playing a sick, twisted game. He moved the cursor to the message and then stopped. He knew he should delete it, but he couldn't seem to make his hand move the mouse any further. He clicked the button and the message opened. There was only one line.

dark here where are you

He carefully set the glass back on the desk. With one hand, he pulled the keyboard closer; with the other, he moved the cursor to 'Reply' and pressed the button. Ignoring the whiskey drops on the keys, he typed:

Who are you? Why are you doing this?

As he stared at the words, an icy ball of fear and dread formed in his stomach. He hit 'Send' and then sat back to wait for the reply, if any. He sipped at his drink while he waited. Two questions played tag in his mind.

Who was at the far end? Why did they want to do something so horrible?

Mark went to the kitchen to refresh his drink. He considered adding an ice cube and then decided against it. Better to have it strong enough to kill the pain – or, at least, to deaden it some. Nothing was going to take it away. Not completely. Probably not ever.

He sipped his drink and then headed back to his office. Setting the glass on a coaster, he slid the office chair forward and sat down. As he expected there was another email from JoannaFletcher227 at the top of the list. A mix of emotion slowly grew within him as he stared at the sender line – dread at what it might contain and anger that some unknown person would be so cruel. After a long moment, he opened it.

dark here where are you

Anger overcame dread as he leaned forward, clicked 'Reply,' and began to type.

Listen you sick bastard. I don't find this a bit funny. I find this cruel and in poor taste. If you're trying to scare me by pretending to be Joanna's ghost, give it up. I don't think they have internet in the beyond. She's dead. Leave me alone.

He clicked on the 'Send' button and sat back. He jerked the glass from the table, ignoring the liquid that sloshed over the back of his hand, and drank deeply. He stared at the screen as time crept. Just as he thought it was over, that whoever it was had finished their game, a new message appeared. Dreading what it contained, he positioned the cursor and clicked the mouse.

dark here cuddlecat where are you im scared

The cold in his belly spread throughout his body. Cuddlecat. That was Joanna's pillow name for him – something no one knew but she and Mark. It couldn't be one of her friends. She had none. That was a big part of the problem. She had built her entire world around him until the weight of it suffocated him.

His hand moved slowly toward the keyboard to type a reply and then stopped. Another message appeared in the inbox. Instead, he reached for the mouse and opened the new email.

cant be dead cuddlecat feel cold see dark

This can't be happening, he thought. *It can't really be her.*

Instead of replying he went to the kitchen to fix another drink. As he poured the whiskey into the glass, he thought back over the events after the break up.

*

She'd had too many possessions – furniture, appliances, knick-knacks, clothes – to just leave. He allowed her to stay while she made arrangements for a rental truck. Her folks had come up to help her pack; he stayed with friends to avoid any confrontations. When she returned his key he ignored the tears in her eyes.

"Are you sure we can't try just one more time?" she begged. "I promise I'll do better. I want to make this work."

He stood silent.

"Can I at least get a goodbye hug?"

He relented and allowed her to embrace him. He tried to ignore her trembling as she sobbed into his shirt. After a long moment she released him and stepped back.

"Take care of yourself," she said softly as she turned and got into her car. His last sight of her was the back of her head as she drove away.

A few weeks later he received an email from her saying that her folks had insisted she move out. She gave no details and he didn't ask for any. Nor did he invite her back, although he felt some guilt that their break up had been the first step in her downfall. He'd received a few more emails telling him that she was living in a shelter and looking for work. Two more weeks had passed with no word.

No word until Dorothy's email.

*

Mark shook his head. He could have prevented Joanna's death. He should have. He should have given her another chance. When her folks kicked her out, he should have told her to come back. If he hadn't been so stubborn, so intractable, none of the rest would have happened.

He took another big drink, refilled the glass, and walked – somewhat unsteadily – back to his office. As he sat down, he saw that yet another email had arrived. He opened it.

killed me cuddlecat

"No!" he screamed at the screen. Yet, even as the word echoed in the tiny room, Mark's mind told him otherwise. If not for him, she would still be alive, probably snoring in their bedroom while he worked to meet another deadline. His hands moved to the keyboard and then withdrew. What could he say? He leaned forward. He clicked on 'Reply.' His fingers danced over the keys.

Not true. It's not my fault. I never meant for anything bad to happen.

He hit 'Send' and leaned back. He raised the tumbler to his lips and drained the contents. He stared at the empty glass and then staggered to the kitchen. He set the glass on the counter and brought the half full bottle back to the office.

Another email was in his inbox.

killed me cuddlecat know what you must do

He replied quickly.

Not my fault.

As his finger clicked 'Send' his mind told him it was a lie. He was as responsible as the mugger who beat her. He put her there as surely as if he'd beaten her himself. He picked up the bottle and took a long drink. As he set it back on the desk, he thought, "I'm guilty. I murdered her."

The next message mirrored his thoughts. There was only one word.

murderer

Mark stared at the word for a long time. Tears trickled down his cheeks but he ignored them as he typed.

I'm so sorry. I didn't mean for this to happen. I don't know what I can do now.

As the message disappeared he took another drink. The reply came back quickly.

you know what to do

He read the words and leaned back in his chair. She was right. He did know what to do. There was only one way to make up for this. He thought for a moment, and then headed for the bathroom.

*

Joanna Fletcher walked into her parent's house. Her depression since the breakup with Mark had been almost debilitating, but she was recovering. She still maintained a hope that they would get back together, but it had been two months and she'd still not heard from him. She'd considered contacting him – if only to make sure he was doing okay – but always thought better of it.

"Hi, Mom," she said as she headed for her room.

"Oh, Joanna. You're home." Dorothy came out of the kitchen, a red and white dish towel in her hands. "Can we talk for a minute?"

"Just a moment. I have to do something on the computer before I forget."

"I'm not sure that's such a good idea. We really need to talk, first."

"Sure thing. I'll only be a minute." Joanna walked to her desk and turned on her computer. As the images filled the screen one story in particular caught her eye.

Noted best-selling supernatural fiction author Mark Edwards was found dead in his Dallas apartment early this morning, apparently from a mixture of alcohol and sleeping pills.

"No!" she screamed as she collapsed into her chair. Sobbing, she read the rest of the article. "Mark, no!" she cried again.

A cruel thought voice – hers, but not hers – cut through her mind like a blade of ice.

Someone had to look out for us, Sweetie, and you were never the strong one.

APIS PRIMATUS

by

Bettina Meister

Thoughts of a Queen

Soon my time will come. I can feel that it will not take much longer. My body is swollen by the burden of its duty. If my servants didn't take care of me, I wouldn't know how to get food – or how to move.

I feel so grateful that my people stand behind me and support me. Yes, they love me. To know this and that I can rely on them fills me with pride and joy. I am taken up with my duty, just as they can expect me to be. It is an honour to exist for my people and to be honoured by them. Therefore I take care for the survival of our dynasty and give birth to sons and daughters, for this is my duty. *For I am the queen.*

A Last Chance

Randolph Tippet, who was on his way to see the chairman of the Association of Research and Modernism, couldn't believe his luck: Right in front of the prestigious building he met Miss Magnolia Pembroke, daughter of Arthur Pembroke, Chairman of said organization. His friendship with her would assure him entrée into the chairman's office, and thus the chance of presenting his ideas.

"My father is a wonderful man. He will certainly like your plan. He has a keen sense for promising ideas."

Magnolia floated past the security employees of the Association like a summer wind. As he was accompanying the daughter of the chairman of the Association, security allowed him to pass without challenge. Instead, the blue-uniformed men sprang to attention, touched their caps with their right hands, and saluted.

Tippet had been turned out of Arthur Pembroke's office without the least bit of ceremony at least twice already.

"It's a wonderful coincidence that we met, isn't it?" Magnolia chatted away in her unpretentious style.

They first met in a coffee house, where he was the first to help an old relative of Magnolia's who had suffered from a sudden faintness. Tippet was unable to forget her. Afterwards their meetings weren't by accident.

"Yes," he replied, "indeed it is."

Elegantly, she climbed the Thompson Permanent Circulator, which steadily moved up and down in a circle. Using a circulator wasn't easy for a lady in fashionable couture.

She patted his arm, "I guess you will have a great career ahead of you, Randolph. The Association is the right place to begin."

In the anteroom of the chairman's office, Pembroke's secretary, Miss Thornsberry, was surprised to see them.

"I'm looking forward to hearing what he says about your plans," Magnolia's joy was honest and touched him – like every meeting with her did. What if he admitted his feelings for Magnolia and asked for permission to court her?

Tippet thought of his own father, an insignificant weaver whose only possessions were a small, shabby cottage, a loom, and some old furniture. The industrialization of the mechanical loom had eaten away his family's meagre income.

"Don't worry, Father", Tippet murmured, "I will do my best – and someday they will understand."

*

Arthur Pembroke's face hardened to formal courtesy when he realized who was escorting his daughter.

"I've met a good acquaintance at the entrance, father," Magnolia dragged the self-conscious Randolph forward. "You know each other, don't you? Did he tell you of his theory on Biomechnatology already? I believe that…"

Distant thunder interrupted her, followed by a hollow rumble, like offshoots of a wave that reached them even here. She rushed to the window, followed by Tippet, while Arthur took a seat behind his desk as if nothing had happened.

The accident seemed to have happened at the factories by the river. A dirty grey cloud could be seen there. A new bang, quieter than the first, echoed from the same direction.

Noticing how little this touched the elder Pembroke, Randolph's feeling grew that his plans were right.

Another rumble sounded, this time out from the wall opposite the windows. Four tubes protruded out of the wall panelling at head height and ended at waist height.

The hollow shaking became louder. With a swishing sound, air flowed from one tube. A longish capsule slid into a catch tray.

Arthur Pembroke, stood, reached for the flexible, copper-capped glass body, and removed the lid. The odour of an industrial factory spread: combusting-vapour, lubrication oil, and graphite, overlapped by the smells of soot and blaze.

Tippet, who often spent many days in factories, recognised this smell at once. He had no doubts that the pneumatic tube came from the affected factory.

Randolph Tippet observed Pembroke unfold the letter and read it, his face cold and void of emotion. It infuriated Tippet that the chairman, head of the whole empire, appeared so callous. Wasn't it his duty as the "Association family's" head to care for his workers?

When Pembroke finished reading the notice, he dropped the paper on the desk carelessly. It slid over the edge and glided onto the floor.

Pembroke was eager to see his daughter from the room. Magnolia, however, mentioned the guest list for the engagement ball, where she wanted to introduce Tippet to her fiancé, Hubert. Not until Arthur mentioned that Hubert Menowing, his daughter's fiancé, was here in the building, did he manage to make his daughter leave his office.

Engagement.

The word slowly trickled into Tippet's awareness.

When father and daughter turned away, Randolph seized the opportunity to grab the letter. He glanced at the paper and then stuffed it into his pocket. That one glance was enough to reveal that an alarming incident had happened. Although he knew that the Association acted irresponsibly toward its workers, this event strengthened Randolph's opinion that it was time to act.

Pembroke neither offered Randolph a seat nor did he sit down himself. "You used my daughter to achieve admission?" he asked, showing his disdain. "Do you not have the slightest sense of pride, man?"

Tippet knew any attempt to answer would be foolish.

"Shall I reiterate my last discourse? If you'd like Tippet, I will do so with pleasure." He seized Randolph's folder and flung it across the room. It opened. Sheets flew out to settle every which way on the polished floor.

"That's what I think of Biomechnatology, Tippet, and of you in particular. No man in full possession of his senses believes that your ideas of a fusion between man and machine can be realized. Your idols – Darwin, Haeckel, or von Baer, didn't have the slightest understanding about the laws of the real world. And, this applies to you, too. Unlike you, the other three didn't try to interfere in questions of industry and manufacture. You claim to mistrust the attitude and functioning of the Association? Even worse, you indefatigably try to present your pipe-dreams as path-breaking innovations. It's time for you to realize that nobody has any interest in your idées fixe."

Tippet had heard enough. He didn't want to waste another second listening. He had come to his decision, and what would happen from now on was inevitable. Randolph considered gathering the sheets from the ground. The pages were manufactured by a multiplecolor-machine; a small fortune for a poor devil like him.

Not that this was of any importance anymore.

Pembroke continued to harangue him, "And if you dare to bother my daughter anymore, I will make your life a living hell. My daughter has been taught to behave properly. And, I warn you: If you dare to get in the way of her marriage to Hubert Menowing, I will stuff you in one of our high temperature furnaces with my own hands."

He darted to the cushioned door, called his secretary, and shouted for security.

They shoved him out. Randolph stumbled, and then landed firmly on the sidewalk. His worn-out bowler, the only one he had, was gone; his suit no longer presentable, and one of his shoes had been lost somewhere on the stairs. The pain shooting through his body mixed with his rage at Arthur Pembroke, his frustration about Magnolia Pembroke's engagement that put her beyond his reach, and his clarity about the way he had to act from now on.

Tippet recovered his composure. With effort, he picked himself up and limped away.

A Blasted Safe

In his library, Arthur Pembroke downed another glass of whisky. This was supposed to be the evening of Magnolia and Hubert's engagement gala, a formal dance arranged with great care and eschewing all costs.

Yet, the unthinkable had happened: Magnolia had been kidnapped, torn from her home by a stranger, gone without a trace.

"Who is this scoundrel who kidnapped her? And, why don't you hunt him down, Cuthbert?" The whisky glass crashed on the marble tabletop.

Cuthbert Goldfinn, head of the criminal investigation department, pensively puffed at his cigar, "We are doing what we can, Arthur. It isn't clear who might have kidnapped her, three hours after her vanishing."

Hubert Menowing continuously turned the engagement ring. Engraved on the inside were the words: OMNIA VINCIT AMOR (Love defeats all).

"And, there is no doubt, Hubert, that she didn't leave by her own choice?" John Finnegan asked, looking up from his notepad. Inspector Finegan, according to Goldfinn the best investigator of the entire police force, stood one step behind his boss.

"What an idea," Pembroke answered instead of Hubert. "She wouldn't even think about doing something like that. She knows what is expected of her."

"Mister Pembroke, Mister Goldfinn, I have just been informed that a burglary took place at the Association this evening. Mister Pembroke, your office was tossed. Your secretary is at the office and asks for your presence. She said a safe was blasted."

"My office?" Arthur Pembroke, who jumped up at the inspector's words, fell back in his armchair. "She said... the safe was *blasted*?"

"Sir?" Pembroke's butler appeared in the door of the study. "A police officer requests to talk to Mister Goldfinn, sir."

Pembroke nodded to signify that the officer should enter.

The police officer handed Goldfinn an envelope, which he opened hastily. He gazed at the contents and then beckoned to Finegan.

After the inspector saw the paper, Goldfinn asked, "Arthur, do you have enemies?"

Finegan handed the sheet to Pembroke. It was a page from a book, apparently on engineering. He recognized immediately the page came from his own book: *Making the Most of Man-Power*.

Pembroke stared at his friend.

"Well," he paused.

"Actually, we…" he cleared his throat, "the Association… there were letters."

Goldfinn looked from Pembroke to Finegan, then across to Menowing and back to Pembroke.

"Finegan, did you know about this?"

Finegan shook his head.

"Where are these letters, Arthur?"

Pembroke muttered something Goldfinn barely understood. As the words finally registered, the stunned policeman raised his eyebrows, "You burned them? Holy Thunder, Arthur! How in the name of God could you do that? They are evidence!"

"I know," started Pembroke, "but…" His voice faltered, "how could I assume that all of them were serious?"

Goldfinn shook his head and took back the paper. "On the face of it, Arthur, this is exactly the point – exactly why you should have taken them seriously."

Arthur sank into his chair.

Transformation

Magnolia cowered on the small wooden bunk, the only piece of furniture in the room. She neither knew where she was, nor how she got there. The last she remembered were the minutes spent in the garden of her parent's house. It had been a comfortable moment – till someone caught her from behind. She believed she had screamed. She had flailed about wildly. The knuckles of her right hand ached. They were swollen; some even seemed to be broken. She only hoped she'd caused her kidnapper some pain, too.

Her ball gown was terribly inappropriate for this place. She had never been this cold before this ordeal. The room was freezing and damp. In order to cover the upper part of her body, she had removed the underskirts to use as a cloak.

Magnolia hadn't wasted much thought on escape. She had never learned to handle crisis situations. When she realized that she could not escape through the light shaft, and that nobody responded to her cries for help, she simply accepted her situation.

"You are a stupid thing", Magnolia berated herself. "You have no idea how to start a fire, not to mention how to free yourself from these circumstances. In your romantic novels there is always a way out."

The feeble light that filtered in through the light shaft was barely sufficient to find her way to the door, through which she received food and drink or to find the hole in the corner, in which she defecated, and back to the bunk.

At first, she refused the food and drink that was left for her while she slept. She threw the food against the door, dumped it in the hole, or smudged a wall with it – hoping her kidnappers would respond – but nothing happened right away. Punishment wasn't long in coming, however.

The first time, her blanket was missing the following day. Another time, the light shaft was barricaded from outside.

After a short time, thirst defeated her resistance. She began to drink. She wasn't even careful to smell it, or to try a mouthful first. It was simply a relief to feel liquid running down her parched throat. After a while, a heavy tiredness crept over her. She curled up on the bunk and fell asleep. To her surprise she not only discovered a warm blanket after her awakening, but also a filled decanter on an upside-down box.

This was how the system of punishment and reward worked.

Just a Muddle Head

The safe had been blasted weeks ago, but Arthur Pembroke was still furious. A glass of whisky shattered into smithereens against his office window. It wasn't the first.

The sound brought Miss Thornsberry. "Mister Pembroke. Is there anything I can do for you?"

"Stop treating me like a steam engine on the verge of exploding!"
Not until she closed the door did he fall in his chair and bury his face in
his hands.

More important than the money, the safe contained the secret con-
tracts with the Royal Monopoly Control – plans for ousting workers'
families in favour of constructing new storage buildings where their
houses stood. The plans were gone, and he didn't dare think what
might happen if the papers ended up in the hands of the leftist worker
coalition. It would be a disaster for the Association. Perhaps the
thieves would hand over the papers in exchange for money. And what
about Magnolia? The police still hadn't come close to her rescue.

Pembroke tore at his hair.

Pembroke jumped to his feet, threw on his camel-hair cloak,
snatched his hat and walking stick, and marched from his office. He
stopped at Miss Thornsberry's desk to tell her he was going to police
headquarters.

*

Cuthbert Goldfinn was just leaving when Arthur entered his office, "Goodness, Arthur, how did you get here so fast? We've just sent
the news to you! And, why *are* you here? There was another explosion."

Pembroke looked at his friend in surprise, "I came to speak to
you. What news do you have?"

Goldfinn took his bowler from the coat hook and snatched Pembroke's arm, "I think you should come with me."

During the drive, Goldfinn explained to his friend what had happened.

The destruction proved severe enough that the factory would be
out of service for quite some time. There had been no warning. A lead
worker reported that he had observed a man handing out leaflets in

front of the factory while urging the workers of that shift to bear their families in mind and go home.

There was no worthwhile description of the man; everything about him was average – average size, hair, weight, not even a recognizable accent. Everyone believed him to be a member of the labour party and paid no attention to him. It was only because two of the huge press rolls had broken down that most workers were outside of the building when the explosion occurred.

John Finegan, the police officer in charge of the investigations, discovered a piece of the explosive device, clearly indicating that these incidents were well-directed attacks.

Drinking and Eating

For the first time in what felt like weeks, Magnolia wasn't cold. She found clothes in her cell that morning, after she finally had eaten something the night before. She had been hungry because she had refused all cooked food since her arrival. She couldn't bear it any longer. It was only a soup, but the aroma of the stock, the warm meat... never before had something so simple tasted so good.

The wool dress scratched at the small hairs on her arms, legs, and back. Tiny hair grew on nearly all parts of her body. She hadn't noticed them at first. The darkness, the cold, the lack of food... yes, those must be the reason.

Magnolia pulled up the skirt and rubbed the hairs. They were yellowish-brown, which she found very surprising, since the small hairs on her arms usually were blond. These were hard and coarse. They also began to... tousle. That word seemed to describe it best.

She stood and paced up and down in her room. In place of water, she was now receiving some type of juice that made her more and more restless. Her body seemed to be confused; she couldn't describe it in another way. The beverage was delicious – refreshing, sweet as honey, and satisfied her thirst like nothing else she knew.

The Master of Bees

Randolph Tippet drew back his left hand just before the automatic welding arm reached him. He laughed, a sound he rarely made. The welding sparks danced over his skin, leaving some burns. For Tippet, they were an engineer's accolade.

He put the welding tip back in place; another bullet tube was complete. Tippet threw the tube into a tank of water, in which a dry chemical was dissolved. The hot metal hissed when it touched the solution.

Tippet observed how the parts, where metal would be melded with human tissue, changed colour: First red, then blue. This indicated that the chemical reaction was finished.

He put a new metal cylinder on the rod. Again Randolph activated the foot pedal to set the machine into operation, and another bullet tube was prepared. He turned away, switched off the main power supply, and went across to the clean room where he prepared for his unification with Magnolia Pembroke.

He had wished for a personal encounter, yet under the circumstances, he had to resort to obtaining the germ cells of his beloved Magnolia, which he would combine with his sperm. The list of applications he had compiled especially for her was attached to the wall next to his desk. Soon she would be ready for the procedure – and ready for her new duty. Only a few days remained until the second transformation level would be sufficiently prepared.

So far he had entered her room only while she was sleeping, not daring to show himself to her. He had no doubts that she would appreciate his plans. She had been interested in Biomechnatology from the very moment he had told her about it in the coffee house.

The hours in the café were special. He was always thrilled by the subtle aroma of her perfume. He customarily smelled of oil, disinfectant and the chemical fluids with which he worked.

When he brought warm clothing to her room the night before, he admired the fine coating of hair which had developed on her neck and cheeks. The longing to touch her naked hairy legs gnawed at him, made his desire to be close to her frustrating beyond measure. But the moment was coming; she would be his queen. She would suffer no pain during her last transformation.

And then his children would fly out, to take revenge on Arthur Pembroke and all the members of the Association. Thus he would prove that his process of wedding human tissue and metal to create a new being was viable.

Magnolia had pleased him by eating the food he had left for her. He hoped she enjoyed the reward of her obedience. There would be a new reward today: Books about their common interest – Biomech-natology.

It was wonderful.

The Revelation

Magnolia raised her eyes and gazed at the book, which she found that morning, together with a candle. The light wasn't strong, the candle flickered. Biomechnatology? She moved the book back and forth, until sufficient light fell on the open pages. She turned to the second page, where title and author were mentioned:

Biomechnatology
Or:
Doctrine About the Evolutionary Memory of Humans and Their Transformation
By Randolph Tippet
Dedicated to his muse and companion, Magnolia

She read the lines again and again. She could comprehend the letters; she could form words out of them. But, the meaning escaped her.

As she thumbed through the book, she was drawn in by a marked passage concerning a confused description of breeding bee soldiers.

They should be built of flesh, fibres and muscles, which were joined to metal components.

"Oh my god," Magnolia gasped. "This is abnormal."

Horrified, she read on, again and again coming upon words or sentences she found particularly disgusting. Burying her face in her hands, she allowed the book to fall to her lap and slide to the ground. The incomprehensible horror of her destiny suddenly became clear. The small hairs on her body, which became more and more hard, coarse, suddenly made sense, as did her now increasingly swollen abdomen.

Randolph Tippet – nobody else could be her kidnapper – had created a demonic plan.

She started to cry without restraint.

Explosion in the Power Station

The annual festivities celebrating Thomas Newcomen's birthday started with the familiar howl of the factory sirens. Newcomen had been the engineer of the first working steam engine in 1712. It was to his glory that they celebrated his birthday with a nationwide holiday. Production in the factories was halted to allow the non-essential workers to participate in the festivities. The engines were lowered to minimum operating capacity, so fewer workers were needed.

At first, the detonation was assumed to be a firecracker shot off early. Only after the fire siren blared and flames burst from the production halls did it become obvious that there had been some sort of accident in the factories.

John Finegan was in charge of the investigations. He didn't allow any clean-up work to start. With the exception of the police, nobody was allowed to access the scene of the explosions. Several times the inspector was seen poking around in the heaps of rubble in search of evidence. Hubert Menowing was at his side most of the time, hoping to help in any way or to find a clue about Magnolia's whereabouts.

Finegan stooped to one knee, pushed aside some ashes, and reached for something. Holding the object carefully between two fingers, he wondered how this thing caught his eye. He rotated it and brought it close to his face. It was a disk, about 10 centimetres in diameter, something he had never seen before. The find was interesting enough to continue the search in this area. Finegan started moving the ashes around again.

"What's that, Finegan?" Hubert tried to see what Finegan had found, just as Finegan bowed down again to pick up something else.

"I have to submit this to the Chief, first," Finegan growled and wrapped the two objects in a handkerchief before putting it in his pocket. Finegan glanced at Menowing. "If my memory doesn't betray me, then this is…" he corrected himself, "…*was* the first factory of Arthur Pembroke."

Hubert Menowing affirmed this.

"Then this factory was the source of chairman Pembroke's wealth?"

"Yes," Hubert's answer was short. Then he added, "Do you think this is associated?"

For a moment Finegan looked at the young engineer silently. Then he rose, cleaned his dirty fingers on the fabric of his trousers, straightened his eyeglasses, and murmured something. A moment later he turned and departed, leaving Hubert Menowing perplexed and confused. Finegan himself was on the way to the senior police medics already, guarding the find carefully.

The Hunt Begins

"Now, Doctor Monegan, what do you think? Are my assumptions correct?" Inspector Finegan leaned toward the doctor across the examination table.

Monegan had examined the finds, cut off parts, placed them in liquids, which changed colours – or didn't. Finally the doctor placed the disk and the spiky something under a microscope. Now and then the doctor took notes, almost without taking his eyes from the specimen.

"I have never seen anything like this in the course of my career," he growled. "Amazing, really amazing."

He looked up and met Finegan's gaze, "and where, did you say, that you found it?"

Finegan related how he had discovered the disk and the huge spike while searching for evidence at the burned-out factory hall.

"When I found it, the spike was stuck in the disk, yet it fell off when I picked it up. So I poked around some more."

Doctor Monegan took the spike out of the microscope and placed it in his palm, "It looks very much like the stinger of a bee. You know about the barbed hook of bees' stingers. Yet, there is no way that such a huge stinger came from a natural bee."

At the Coalface

Another factory went up in flames. Three weeks had passed since the last incident. The destruction was more profound this time. The target of this latest attack was a facility under the aegis of the Association that produced the raw materials used in manufacturing at other locales. The destruction had been complete, razing the buildings to the ground. Once more an unknown man had passed out handbills before the shift. Significantly more workers than last time took the message to heart and left the site. The security service had been on alert, yet they had little chance to prevent what was happening that day.

According to witnesses, it began with a small buzzing in the air, like a tremendous swarm of insects flying over the factory.

One of the men could hardly stop the tremor in his voice, trying to talk about the aggression when the police interrogated them. "We, we did... it was... I..." the man's voice broke away, his whole body quaking.

His colleague, who seemed to have stronger nerves, continued the report: "They came down to the factory area from the mountains.

When we saw them coming, it was too late already. It was humming like a fan on high."

Goldfinn insisted on questioning the victims himself, with Finegan standing beside his boss like a regular policeman, taking notes.

"You said it was bees. How can that be?"

"Dunno, sir. How should we know?" Confused, the man looked from Goldfinn to Finegan, whom he had been talking to before.

Goldfinn tried again, "Please, just describe for me what you saw."

The two men fell silent and stared at their dirty, chapped hands.

"Now, go on," Goldfinn wasn't very patient.

"Hm…, sir. Well, sir," one of them finally began, "they was gigantic bees, a lot bigger than normal, and eyes burning like fire in 'em."

Finegan frowned and made a note: Bees have faceted eyes – check facts.

"Some of them had round bombs an' long fuses in their hands. They dropped the bombs on the buildings."

Again, Finegan made a note.

"And others were like, mad, y' know? All dashing through the halls and shooting the 'coves with these cannon tubes in their bodies."

More and more quickly the words gushed from them.

"Some went flying straight to the chemical tanks. Over 'ere they destroyed all they could as well."

"And then some were after… us."

"They had mighty huge wings," the colleague chimed in, "as long as their bodies. And helmets."

"And," the first worker continued, "and they grinned like it was fun. And when I thought they had us, then they just backed off and whoosh – away. Just so."

With Finegan's insights after the last attack, he saw little reason to doubt what the men had said. The search in the scrap metal, ash and rubbish was obviously not yet completed.

"Sir," Finegan bent to Cuthbert Goldfinn, "I think you are doing great. Do you think it might help if we sent these men home for now?"

Goldfinn did what John Finegan expected him to: He declared, as if it had been his own idea, that the two workers should go home, since it would not be very helpful to continue the questioning right then. Perhaps they would remember more later on.

The two men, obviously relieved, walked away.

Tracking the Villain

Professor Casparius, the well-known apiologist, who was not only an expert in the study of bees and beekeeping, but also an active, passionate apiculturist, received them in his wild hodgepodge of a study. All shelves, tables, even stools and arm chairs, were covered with papers, books, statues, and taxidermied animals. He offered glasses of port to both Dr. Monegan and John Finegan. Monegan accepted happily; Finnegan declined as he was on official business.

"You sent me notice, dear gentlemen, that you need my help in solving a crime," Casparius said as he sipped from his glass of wine.

The professor was exactly the type of scientist Finegan expected: A little eccentric, dressed in a brocade smoking jacket. He had an awkward manner of speaking.

"Indeed, my honourable colleague."

Finegan smiled as he listened to Doctor Monegan.

Monegan related to the Professor all that had transpired thus far, listing for him the interrelations and correlations he believed to exist. Finegan would have been able to tell the whole story in a third of the time. During these elucidations Monegan not only presented the disk and spike Finegan found, but also findings from the last attack.

Casparius' eyes grew wider with every "foretaste," as he called it. He sent his assistant, Miss Fulton, scurrying about every few minutes to get a slide for the microscope or to look up the information of various bee cultures in a specialist's publication. After a short time, the professor was convinced that these were altered bees, mixed with human biological sources.

Finegan was a little disappointed that Casparius didn't want to come with them right away, although he was totally excited about this find.

A Toast

Randolph Tippet was sitting in his wing chair, which had been carried to Magnolia's room by a servant.

Magnolia seemed to feel well, even though she moved very little. She tolerated the offered nutrition well. The brood was strong, and each new generation developed magnificently. Magnolia had undergone development as well herself. Starting as a young woman, she had become a responsible hive mother. The grubs she birthed with delightful and necessary regularity became grand and excellent beemen. After passing through adolescence with astonishing speed, they could – just as Tippet had planned – be formed into soldiers. By adding the metal supplement at the right time, they became parts of his army.

Tippet was immensely proud of his creations. They were strong. Losses in the growth actuator were small. And, except for a few who had to be left behind dead on the battle-grounds, they were doing an excellent job.

He raised his glass, filled with an exceptionally expensive whiskey thanks to the haul from Pembroke's safe, and toasted to Magnolia. As always her wonderful violet eyes looked at him with craving for affirmation of a job well done.

"You are a wonderful companion, dearest Magnolia. I drink to you," He raised the glass and took a deep gulp.

In the eyes of the being that once was Magnolia Pembroke, a tear appeared.

At the Patent Office

The next day Randolph closed the door to the part of the house where Magnolia and the grubs lived. Nothing should disturb them. They should eat and develop. Providing for the family and protecting them from harm were his tasks. And then there was something else: His conviction that society could no longer exist the way it was.

The technical description of his development had been edited according to the guidelines of the patent office. He carried the draft sheets with him, as well as all necessary forms.

After his appointment at the patent office, where he handed in his papers and paid his fees, he was ready to begin the next phase of his plan. He needed to find investors, factory premises, and construction of machinery. Only then could he carry his plan forward completely. Everything was planned in detail. And – with everything developing as desired – the opening would be possible within a year.

Thanks to the streamlined bus route he arrived at the patent office in the governmental district in less than an hour. This building did not just contain the patent office. It held the admission office for factories with particularly high energy needs and the registration office for certified engineers. Entering the building through the revolving door, he pulled the bundle of papers from the inside of his coat. He noticed that there were a number of police officers inside the building; one leaving by way of the same revolving door he entered. Tippet showed no sign of tension despite the uniformed forces all around.

He climbed the stairs to the second floor, entered the left wing, and found room 43B. On his way he passed another hallway. Several policemen were busy stacking cardboard boxes. One of them lost his grip on a box. It fell to the floor, bursting open. Files fell out, scattering across the floor.

A look at the sign on the hall showed Tippet which department was there: The Registration Office for Engineers archives. Were they searching for him?

Tippet felt no urge to flee; why should he? He had done nothing wrong. He merely followed his ideas. The day would come when people recognized that he was working to better humankind. And then he could talk openly about Magnolia's transformation

Tippet took a deep breath, knocked on the door of the Office for Patent Acceptance, and entered.

"Mister Jones," he smiled courteously, smiling broadly, hand outstretched, "My name is Tippet. Randolph Tippet. I have an appointment with you."

Herbert Jones took off his glasses. He rubbed his eyes with the other hand and tried to steady his stomach, which began to revolt as he listened to Tippet's plans. As soon as the small, insignificant-looking man in the ill-fitting suit had left, Jones ran to the window. He threw it open hastily and stuck his head out. Despite the flue of the adjacent factory, he needed fresh air. His head clear and his stomach somewhat calm, he grabbed the strange man's papers from the desk and went down the hall to where the police were working.

The Search for the Hive

Seven people crowded the police meeting room: Goldfinn, Finnegan, Arthur Pembroke, who brought Menowing along, Dr. Monegan, Professor Casparius, and his assistant, Miss Fulton. Finegan, Menowing, Goldfinn, and Dr. Monegan were the only ones present officially working on the case. Professor Casparius and Miss Fulton were there as experts.

"To find the hive, you must follow the bee," Professor Casparius looked around the small, crowded room. The listeners all reacted differently, each according to his temperament.

Arthur Pembroke jumped up and began talking to Goldfinn fervently, who, in turn, looked at John Finegan, waiting for his response. Finegan fervently wished he had been able to prevent the presence of the Chairman *and* Goldfinn. He was sure that involving Pembroke in the investigation was dangerous. Arthur Pembroke was not the kind of man who took direction from others. He also tended to act rashly. Finegan could see that the man was forming a plan in his head. It would be useless to try to convince Goldfinn that this meeting would result in a catastrophe. With the information they were being given, there was no way that a man like Arthur Pembroke would leave the investigating to the police. He was used to taking charge, giving orders, and having those orders followed.

"This means that we are dealing with an abductor who is breeding an army of soldiers, reconstructed as monstrous war machines, and built for the sole purpose of hunting me," he marched up and down with heavy steps, "and this... man... has my daughter in his power?"

He stopped in front of Finegan and looked at him indignantly, "Why haven't you arrested that riffraff by now? How long do you plan to wait? Do you have any idea how much money I have lost thanks to these attacks? And, I would really like to get my daughter back!"

Inspector Finegan ignored him, the best thing to do under the circumstances, and suggested that in this meeting with the Professor they would think of how to best proceed. Only the Professor had any idea of what needed to be done: Find the beehive. The others gathered around the large, oval conference table to discuss how best to proceed with his plan.

"You do not have many options, my dear sirs," Professor Casparius' words were friendly, yet he seemed to be hiding something.

Cuthbert Goldfinn lit a cigar and murmured between puffs, "He would not use her as a midwife. That would not be very nice."

The Professor kept a straight face as he looked at the chief. He decided to elaborate on his thoughts, "If it is your intention to save the dear Magnolia from her fate as a laying machine for monsters, you should act quickly.

Finegan cleared his throat, seeing the faces of Pembroke and Menowing, "*Hrmph.* Well. Professor, I agree with you, all in all. We didn't find Tippet in his home. We don't know where he is. The

papers he handed in showed his known address. And, without inter-
rogating him, we will not be able to find the beehive – as you call it –
in sufficient time. With Miss Pembroke's family present, I do not want
to go into more detail."

One could see in Arthur Pembroke's face as it slowly dawned on
him what his daughter was facing.

"But, you can't possibly mean that we will be sit here idle, waiting for another attack," Arthur Pembroke harangued.

For the first time Hubert Menowing spoke, his voice carrying the
ring of conviction, "Whatever is necessary, Mr. Pembroke, sir. Whatever is necessary, I will be with you."

Finegan didn't react, knowing Pembroke would take the young
man at his word without even knowing what they would face

"Well, sirs," Goldfinn thumped the table with the flat of his hand.
"Then let us talk facts."

Menowing didn't understand, "But, we do not know where the
hive is."

This time it was John Finegan who answered, and it was apparent
that he was pleased with his success, "Brace yourselves and come with
me, please." He stood and moved toward a door, "Right this way," he
opened it, "but, please do not touch anything."

The Professor bade the others enter first. Goldfinn, who already
knew what awaited them, proceeded with assurance. Miss Fulton
brought up the rear, ready as always to do the Professor's bidding.
Pembroke and Menowing were the only ones who didn't know what
to expect. Menowing, the young hero, felt his gorge rising.

There was a thing lying on an upholstered bench – a thing that
those seeing it tried to dismiss as an impossibility: the body of a bee-
soldier. It had been found seriously injured, barely holding on to life,
and it was only due to the expertise of Professor Casparius, Dr. Monegan, and Miss Fulton that it lived.

The workers who had knocked it from the air had not bothered to
treat their captive with any kindness or gentleness. One of its four

back legs had been torn out, two more were broken. One of its arms was missing. The helmet, which lay on another table, had been taken away to examine the skull, as had a metal plate that covered the bee-soldier's stomach and rib cage. The wings looked like milk glass, interwoven with silver threads, and glinted in the light. Although Finegan had seen this human bee several times, he still was repelled and yet fascinated at the same time.

"Professor, do you think this... thing," Pembroke was the first to overcome his horror, "might be able to lead us to the hive?"

Professor Casparius looked doubtful, "I assured myself a few hours ago that it will live. I am not sure it will be able to get back to its hive."

"What do you mean?" Pembroke insisted on an answer, raising his fist aggressively. It seemed as if he were trying to threaten the Professor into supplying an answer.

Finegan felt wary. The man was up to something.

"The bee-soldier will need a few more days of strengthening. We found he responded particularly well to Royal Jelly, mixed with a small amount of finely minced meat."

Professor Casparius nodded to Miss Fulton to furnish more details.

"Usually a bee has a range of about three-quarters of a statute mile. We do not yet know the range of these man-bees. Considering the size, alterations, the wingspan...."

"This means," Finegan added, "that it will take a few more days to help the bee-soldier to get stronger to make sure it can cover the distance, right?"

"And then, we begin Project 'Back to the Hive,' and we will have them," Goldfinn added with grim delight.

"And till then – we wait?" Pembroke remained stubborn.

"You have to understand, Mr. Pembroke," the Professor struggled to make him understand, "we know nothing about this being and his nature. We do not know how to gauge its health. We cannot answer your question."

With an angry jerk, Arthur Pembroke wrenched the sheet from the being's head. He stiffened as he saw the open eyes of the bee-soldier. They were the same violet hue as his daughter's eyes.

Pembroke's Decision

Nobody saw the two men who walked the side roads. It was so early in the morning that workers had not yet started their day. The two men didn't talk. One – Arthur Pembroke – clutched a set of keys in his jacket pocket, courtesy of Goldfinn. Pembroke knew – without speaking a single word – that Goldfinn approved of Pembroke's decision to act. When he had seen the violet eyes of his daughter in the head of the monster, he knew exactly what he had to do. Pembroke had seen enough to know there was no time to lose.

It was easy to find the receiving entrance of the police station's canteen. From there they planned to find the windowless room where the bee soldier was kept. They locked the door from the inside before turning on the lights. The creature was awake, in comparatively good shape, and in chains. Pembroke had the keys to these chains. Pembroke took the sheet from the beast's head and watched it wake. Pembroke's heart began to beat faster. Facing the fact that he would have to touch this monstrous creature, he was almost overcome by nausea.

Involuntarily he talked to it, "Don't worry. There is no need to be afraid. We are here to set you free."

If this being, no matter whether human, bee, or metal, could understand him at all, he didn't know.

Hubert, the second man, began to remove the chains that held the human bee to its sickbed. The creature felt its chains loosen and began to move its arms and legs as if to relieve the pins and needles feel of their having been asleep. Then other muscles in the body began to shrug. Finally, the bee-soldier moved its head.

"We can't attach the pipes," Menowing said, pointing to holes in which threads were tapped. They looked like the empty hollows of dead eyes.

"Who cares about that?" snorted Pembroke, "Just make sure to attach the metal shield to its stomach."

Menowing was an engineer, so it was no real task to fasten the screws. The wings were still fastened to the body, and Pembroke certainly wasn't of a mind to unfasten them at this point.

"So," Arthur Pembroke whispered into the bee soldier's ear, "we will set you free. I will lead you to a place where you can take off, and then you can return to your hive and tell them that we are no danger for you. There is no need to attack us. Come."

With these words Pembroke placed the helmet on the bee-man's head and turned to Menowing, "Ready? Let's go."

Together they heaved the creature from its sickbed and placed it on the floor as tenderly as possible. When Menowing saw it crawling like the injured bee that it was, he felt a sudden urge to beat it to death. They placed a leash around the creature's neck.

Pembroke was surprised that the creature showed no urge to escape or to kill him; in fact, it raised no resistance whatsoever. Maybe it had understood Pembroke's whispered words after all. With the added burden of the bee-soldier, the way back through the building to the street seemed twice as long as their entry had been.

"Hurry up," Pembroke hissed to Hubert, whose task it was to secure their back, "We need to get out as soon as we can!"

Toward the Mountains

Driving like a lunatic, Arthur Pembroke steered his big, steam-powered car through a slowly awakening city. They reached the eastern outskirts of town as they headed toward the mountains on a traffic artery. He was relieved to leave the business centre where it would be impossible at this time of the day to lead the creature to where it could take flight.

The monster had been an obedient animal. It had not tried to escape or attack during the walk in town. It was hard to imagine that this creature had held bombs in its hands, killed Pembroke's dreams, and murdered his workers. And then, Magnolia's eyes and the horror of what they might find at Tippet's beehive filled Pembroke's mind.

They found the launch point Pembroke had planned to use – a flat overlook facing the east and overlooking a shallow valley. They released the creature without fanfare. At first, it appeared that its injuries might prove too much to permit it to fly. After a moment, however, it stumbled toward the edge and leaped. Both men's breath caught as the creature dipped, but they exhaled and ran back to the car once the bee-man rose unsteadily into the air. They followed the creature from below, Hubert watching the monster's progress and feeding directions to Pembroke.

Townhouses gave way to plant nurseries and orchards. The houses were remote from the streets, settled deeply within their grounds. Their guide was flying particularly low, weak without a doubt. Pembroke didn't care. At times it seemed to sink, then pull itself together to continue on its way. The further east they went, the louder its drone became. These sounds and its unexpected slow speed made it even easier for Pembroke and Menowing to follow. The fluorescent liquid that Pembroke had used to paint the metal shield and the underside of its body seemed unnecessary.

The sun had not yet begun to climb over the mountains when Pembroke glanced at the odometer on the dashboard. They were about five miles from the city centre. "It can't be far now, Hubert."

Throughout its flight, the winged warrior had more or less followed the street. Now it changed direction slightly, veering left.

"Oh, my God!" Menowing shouted, his voice shrill and tense. "It's heading over there. And, it's going down, descending."

Pembroke's victorious shout resounded through the car: *"Yes! That damned nutty Professor was right!"*

Hubert repeated the Professor's words: "As long as the hive hasn't moved and the bee creature's brain is not seriously injured, it will always find its way back."

Indeed, the monster had turned toward a single farmstead. A: a junction where a narrow dirt lane lead to the farm from the main road, Pembroke reduced speed and turned left. The farm, whose roofs could hardly be seen, was about a ten minute walk away. The bee-soldier headed directly toward the farm.

Pembroke parked the car. Before leaving, both men pulled heavy-weight work suits over their clothes for added protection. Pembroke congratulated himself for his smart move and told Menowing to come with him. They left the car, armed themselves, and followed the bee-soldier's path. Walking under the trees that lined the lane, they were sure that nobody could see them from the house. It was too dark and the leaves covered them from above. Neither man saw any signs of security measures to the right or left.

Both had agreed on a plan. They would surprise Tippet and his ugly beasts. They would get inside, rescue Magnolia, and then blow the whole thing to hell, including Tippet and all of his machinery

When the farm was in sight, they stopped for a moment to take a last deep breath. In addition to the weapons they carried, they had flare guns – Veri pistols – to signal the police after they found Magnolia – and killed Tippet and every creature in the nest.

During the last weeks Pembroke had spent most of his nights thinking, and trying to decide what to do if they found Magnolia in a state of something beyond imagination. He was aware that she might no longer be his child, but some horrible creature that had nothing in common with the Magnolia he knew. He didn't share these thoughts with Menowing. A man of decision, he knew he might have to put an end to whatever Magnolia might have become.

The Final Battle

In the middle of the clearing stood the farm house, the barns and stables spread out to either side and behind. No machinery was visible, no hint of farm equipment.

"Do you smell that?" Pembroke asked, sniffing the air. "A sweet scent."

"Yes, I noticed it before. Like..." he paused for a moment, "...like honey!"

"Exactly", Pembroke agreed. "We are where we need to be. And over there is what we are looking for."

The wounded bee-soldier was moving toward a gate on the left side of the barn. They heard a scratching sound, and then it was gone. The scout had disappeared into its hive.

Arthur Pembroke turned to his companion, "Menowing, it is up to you whether you go any further or not. I will not think less of you if you decide to call the police and wait for them. We might have to do things that are beyond our imagination."

Hubert gripped his weapon tighter, a modern semi-automatic rifle, "I will not let you go on your own, sir. I will be right beside you."

Pembroke nodded. The last part of their rescue action began. Pembroke removed a switchblade from his boot and a revolver from under his jacket at his back, "This is Tippet's laboratory. Here we will find this mad engineer and his monster bees."

"And, hopefully, Magnolia," added Menowing, "and if not, I will beat his brains out of him till he tells me where she is."

Pembroke hesitated for a moment. He was impressed by Menowing's determination, yet hoped the young man would not lose his resolve at the sight of Magnolia if she, too, had become a monster.

Nothing opposed their way to the main entrance. They kept close to the wall of the left building and moved beneath the shadow of the overlapping roof. More and more clearly they could hear the buzzing and humming of huge bee wings. They were like a distant motor constantly working. They had no idea of the number of bee monsters this Tippet had already bred.

"Tippet, you devil!" Pembroke chewed the name of the detested man and spat it out. The industrialist would never have guessed that this innocuous little man could plot something like this, let alone carry it to fruition.

A movement behind him startled Pembroke. He turned quickly to find himself facing a bee-soldier. It held Menowing in its hands, shaking the young man like a jointed doll. Pembroke grabbed his knife firmly, and, without hesitation, stabbed the only area he could think of – one of the eyes.

The injured being emitted a piercing shriek. The rupture of a violet eye so identical to Magnolia's, only added to his fury. With all his strength, he drew the knife back and tried, again, to blind the bee-soldier. Miraculously, he succeeded. Still shrieking, the devilish creature let go of Menowing, who fell to the ground and remained there motionless.

Pembroke backed off to get out of reach of the-bee soldier's arms. A few steps away was the rifle Menowing had brought with him, but dropped when the creature attacked. Pembroke reached for it, charged, and shot without aiming. The bee warrior was thrown against the bricks of the barn's wall and slid to the floor, dying.

Pembroke felt relieved, like an immense weight was lifted from his shoulders. It was possible to kill them. They could be defeated! He knew that they could be – the wounded one they followed indicated that – but to actually do it, to see it with his own eyes, gave him more confidence.

"Menowing!" Pembroke hurried to his fellow fighter, not knowing whether or not he was still alive. Arthur quickly saw that the young man was dead, likely from a broken neck. Pembroke, with a sudden feeling of sympathy, stroked the dead man's hair, and then began to search through Menowing's jacket, trying to find the Veri Pistol. He didn't know if the noise of the fight had alarmed the other soldiers. Looking around, he reassured himself that no bee-soldier had entered the farm yard yet.

It was too early to shoot off the signal, wasn't it? They sent notice to Finegan and Goldfinn that they should look out for their flare, the signal that they had found the hive. Pembroke's eyes darted to the farm buildings, down to Menowing's corpse, and back to the pistol in his hand. He glanced at the rifle next to the dead bee-soldier. What should he do?

Then he made up his mind and fired the signals. One, two, three: The flares shot into the air and exploded in silver cascades, visible in the daylight sky. Dropping the flare gun, Pembroke grabbed the rifle, stuffed the knife back in the belt of his trousers, and began to sneak toward a small door he had spotted next to him, knowing that when the police arrived he might either be dead or captive.

Thoughts of a Queen II

I hear a commotion among my people. I sense one of my soldiers has come back from a fight. I feared I had lost him, but now he is back. He has been dancing the dance of food he found. It is such a marvellous dance. I hear my people rejoice. In a few moments they will come and feed me. I am thankful for how they take care of me. The food smells wonderful – fresh blood and meat, carefully prepared for me by my master.

UNDER THE BED

By

Shirley Meier

I've killed my Mummy.

I'm crouched in the hallway, staring at my bedroom door. My closed bedroom door. I'm staring at the dark under the bottom edge where the light should be. Mummy turned off the light. There's crunching noises coming from inside.

Mummy never liked that I see things in my bedroom. Under the bed. In my closet. Behind the door.

Even hiding in the cracks and shadows of window edges. Those have teeth all along their bodies. The thing under the bed… it had baby teeth when I first saw it. When the thing grew grownup teeth, it spit the monster baby teeth onto my rug. I saw them… they turned to smoke and went away when the sun hit them in the morning.

I've been saying I don't like the dark for a long time. I had two night lights and I still couldn't sleep. I really, really saw the monsters, the boogey men.

The monsters sang songs… made up songs about the horrible things they were going to do to me.

The noises in my bedroom are getting squishier.

I killed Mummy. They are eating her.

I told Mummy about the boogey men today. She made me. She came home from work and sat me down and we had cookies and milk and she said the Doctor Lady at the school said she needed to talk to me. But the Doctor Lady keeps saying that monsters aren't real. I told Mummy I wasn't making things up. I told Mummy that I'm staying awake because Mummy might come in and turn out the light. They can't eat me if the light is on. I can see them and they scare me and I wet the bed.

The monsters in my room are real. I can see them. I cried and told Mummy and she listened and then said, "All right. I am going to fix this." She got up and went upstairs with me running after her. And I tried to stop her. It was dark already and I knew they'd be in there. I knew they'd be in my room and I screamed and cried and she opened the door with the hall light making a safe spot, a safe knife of light into my room. She stood in the door.

"No Mummy, no! Don't go in there!"

She reached over and flipped the light on. I had to stay down the hall outside the bathroom. Snuffy, my puppy, was hiding in Mummy's bedroom and he was whining.

"See," she went inside, "nothing here." She poked under the bed with a broom and in the closet, but the lights were on.

"Mummy, please!"

She stood up and smiled at me and I love her and I'm scared for her. She said, "Wait a minute." And then she closed the door. She turned the light out, I could see the crack of light under the door go away and I screamed as loud as I could, but my screaming didn't cover the noise of the growling.

There's a lot of banging and growling and howling and crashing and breaking things. Then the crunching noises. The chewing noises. The boogey men are eating my Mummy and then they're going to come out and do all the things that they sang to me… and it's going to hurt a lot.

I stare at the door, shaking. I'd have to go closer to my bedroom door to get to the top of the stairs and I can't. Snuffy whines behind me, comes up to me where I'm crouched and I put my arms around him. We're gonna die. I wet myself as the doorknob turned.

The door opens and the light is on. It's not the boogey men. It's Mummy. Her hair is wild and she looks tired and is covered in stuff that looks like red and green paint. She wipes her mouth and says, "It's all right, lovey. Monsters are no match for mummies. You'll find out one day when you have a little girl of your own. Nothing… *nothing* is a match for an angry mummy."

ABOUT THE AUTHORS

C. Dean Andersson: Dean's *I Am Dracula* is Dracula's favorite vampire novel because the immortal Wallachian Prince Vlad "The Impaler" Drakulya helped write it. Dean's *Raw Pain Max* is the Hungarian Blood Countess Erzebet Bathory's favorite SplatterPunk (heavy metal horror) cult classic for the same reason. Vlad and Erzebet also like Dean's other novels and short stories, including the delicious "Small Brown Bags of Blood," "Mama Strangelove's Remedies for Afterlife Disorders," and the Bram Stoker Award Finalist, "The Death Wagon Rolls on By." Meanwhile, back on the Viking dragonship, Dean's *Bloodsong! Helx3* is an upcoming omnibus e-book from Event Horizons, collecting his Norse fantasy (sword and sorcery) *Warrior Witch of Hel, Death Riders of Hel,* and *Werebeasts of Hel.* Dean is currently writing *Bloodsong! Valkyries of Hel* and *I Am Dracula II.*

You may visit his website at www.cdeanandersson.com.

Nancy Asire: Nancy Asire is the author of four novels, *Twilight's Kingdoms, Tears of Time, To Fall Like Stars* and *Wizard Spawn.* She also has written short stories for the series anthologies *Heroes in Hell* edited by Janet Morris, and *Merovingen Nights,* edited by C.J. Cherryh. Other short stories of hers have appeared in Mercedes Lackey's anthology *Flights of Fantasy,* as well as tales for the Valdemar anthologies. She authored additional short stories for *Lawyers in Hell* and *Rogues in Hell.* She has lived in Africa and traveled the world, but now resides in Missouri with her cats and two vintage Corvairs.

Larry Atchley, Jr.: Larry Atchley, Jr., grew up in Grapevine, Texas, writing stories and poetry since he was a teenager. He became serious about publishing his fiction writing after attending a writers' workshop presented by authors Sarah A. Hoyt and Amanda S. Green in 2010. His first big break came when authors Janet Morris and Chris Morris invited him to join their shared world anthology, *Heroes in Hell.* They accepted "Remember, Remember, Hell in November" for *Lawyers in Hell.* He has stories that were published in the following anthologies in 2012: *Sha'Daa: Pawns,* and *Rogues in Hell,* as well as a poem in the upcoming collection, *A Book of Night.* He is currently working on a couple of fantasy novels. In 2012 Larry was also inducted into the fiction authors group The Fictioneers.

You can read his blog, The Short Pale Writer in the Long Black Coat at www.larryatchleyjr.wordpress.com. You can also see him at various science fiction, fantasy, and literary conventions throughout the year. He lives with his wife, Sussie Atchley, a professional freelance photographer, and his daughter Alina Atchley, an artist and custom jewelry maker. They live with their two terriers, Frodo and Rosie, and two cats, Samwise and Prue in the suburbs of the Dallas/Fort Worth Metroplex, in Texas.

Thomas Barczak: Tom is an Artist, turned Architect, turned Writer, who is finally getting around to finishing those stories he started as a kid. His work includes his debut illustrated novel, *Veil of the Dragon,* along with two illustrated serials for Kindle, *Awakening Evarun (Parts I-VI),* and *Fall of the Chosen* (of which Part I has been released).

Mostly he writes because he can't not. "I write because I want to tell a story that I started way before, with my paintings, with my poetry, and even again before that, sitting around a table with my friends, slaying dragons."

Wayne Borean: Wayne learned how to drive a car at six years old, raced cars, motorcycles, & snowmobiles for years. Barroom brawler, boxer, and he played hockey for years, and had a reputation as a vicious defenseman. Worst case of Testosterone Poisoning you've ever seen… Makes him an atypical geek (he loves computer programming), and an atypical reader, who has become a writer since his body decided to pack it in, and he can't be physically active anymore.

David Conyers: David is an Australian science fiction author residing in Adelaide. With John Sunseri he is the co-author of the Lovecraftian spy thriller collection, *The Spiraling Worm,* and the author of the sequel novella, *The Eye of Infinity,* both of which feature further Harrison Peel tales. He is the editor of the anthology *Cthulhu's Dark Cults,* with Brian M. Sammons the editor of *Cthulhu Unbound 3,* and is a contributing editor for *Albedo One,* Ireland's longest running magazine of speculative fiction, and *Midnight Echo,* the Australian Horror Writers Association official fiction magazine. David's short fiction has appeared in various magazines including *Jupiter, Book of Dark Wisdom, Ticon4, Midnight Echo, Innsmouth Free Press,* and *Andromeda Spaceways Inflight Magazine.* He has also appeared in over a dozen anthologies including *Monstrous, Best New Tales of the Apocalypse, Horrors Beyond, 2008 Award Winning Australian Writing, Scenes from the Second Storey,* and *Macabre.* www.david-conyers.com

Jason Cordova: Jason Cordova did not want to be a writer. He wanted to be many other things, first and foremost a professional baseball player. After that, a teacher, then a professional videogame player. However, with the deck stacked against him (as well as too many injuries to his shoulder, which killed the aspirations of videogaming and baseball), in 2007 he finally accepted the writing gig and sold his first

D ABOUT THE AUTHORS

book three months later. Since then he has had multiple short stories published and more novels in the pipeline.

J. D. Fritz: A mixed martial arts enthusiast and wannabe Derby Girl, Joan Darcy Fritz lives in the Dallas/Ft. Worth Metroplex and supplements her non-existent writing income by fighting crime. No, really.

Richard Groller: Richard is co-author of *The Warrior's Edge* (with Janet Morris and Col. John Alexander), and a contributing author to *The American Warrior* (Janet and Chris Morris, Eds.), and to the *Heroes of Hell* shared universe anthology. Nominated for *Military Intelligence* Professional Writer of the Year in 1986, he has published numerous historical and technical articles in such venues as *Military Intelligence, The Field Artillery Journal, Guns and Ammo,* and *The Journal of Electronic Defense.* As a contributing writer to the *Heroes of Hell* series, he has been published in *Prophets in Hell* and *Lawyers in Hell*, and has two stories accepted for the next two volumes in the series. He is Editor of a volume of dark poetry called *The Book of Night* that will be published by Perseid Publishing in 2012. His short story, *"The Bokor,"* will be published in 2013 in the recently released volume of the *Sha'Daa series* shared universe anthology *Sha'Daa: Pawns.* When not writing, Rich is Director of Business Development for Dilijent Solutions, LLC, a Northern Virginia based defense contractor involved with software and engineering related technical and managerial support for the Department of Defense and Intelligence Community.

Beverly Hale: Bev Hale collects things – books, hats, friends, insults in various languages, recipes, etc. Lately, she has been spending most of her time as a Steampunk artist. However, when she isn't involved with gears, she writes. Bev has written and published in gaming, comics, short stories, a cookbook, a children's book and she even has a fantasy novel, *The Essence of Stone*.

Michael H. Hanson: The son of a U.S. Army Sergeant and a nurse, Michael H. Hanson is the fourth of five children and was born in New York State's Northcountry (a land so frigid and forbidding that at least once a year it is quoted on Winter news broadcasts as "the coldest spot in the nation.") Michael attended Syracuse University, where alongside his filmmaking activities he found a few spare moments to study creative writing and poetry. He graduated from the Newhouse School of Public Communications with a degree in Film Production in 1989. "Autumn Blush," his first volume of poetry, was published by YaYe Books in 2008. "Jubilant Whispers," his second collection of poetry, was published by Diminuendo Press in 2009. His fictional creation, the *Sha'Daa* series, is a shared-world horror anthology (containing the work of 11 writers including himself). A transplanted New Yorker, Michael acquired dual-citizenship with his name being entered into Ireland's Foreign Births Entry Book. A haunted Sagittarian, he presently resides in Piscataway, NJ where he edits engineering society journals for a living, and occasionally dabbles in genealogy research and collecting impressionist oil paintings. He spends his free time spinning both tales of the fantastic and introspective poetry in his small but cozy garden apartment.

John Manning: Born on Halloween, John has always been fascinated by the dark and scary world of horror fiction. His earliest favorites were Edgar Allen Poe, Dostoevsky, and Charles Addams. He discovered his passion for writing in the second grade. Through the years, however, publishers did not share his enthusiasm. As a staff member for fan conventions, he was blessed to meet (and pick the brains of) the likes of Barry Longyear, Robert Asprin, Robert Adams, L. Sprague de Camp, C. Dean Andersson, John Steakley, Jr., Lynn Abbey, Andy Offutt, and Larry Niven. Evidently osmosis works, for in 2011 his first novel, *Black Stump Ridge*, written with his long-time friend, Forrest Hedrick, was published. It has gone on to place tenth in the Editors & Preditors Poll in the best new horror novels for 2011, as well as being placed on the 2011 Nebula Recommended Reading List. His short story, "Disclaimer," appeared in Janet and Chris Morris' *Lawyers in Hell*, released in July 2011. "Showdown at Brimstone Arsenal," appears in the 2012 release, *Rogues in Hell.* He also has a short story, "Asylum," that is part of Michael H. Hanson's *Sha'Daa: Pawns*, released by Perseid Publishing in October 2012. He is currently working on *Levi*, the sequel to *Black Stump Ridge* (with Forrest Hedrick), *Walkabout in Hell*, a spin-off novel from Janet and Chris Morris' *Heroes in Hell*, and *Fear the Reaper*, a vampire novel (with no sparklies). As Editor-in-Chief of Fantom Enterprises, he is also working on two more anthologies, *Terror by Gaslight* and a heroic fantasy collection entitled *Heroes All.*.

Shirley Meier: Over the years, solo and with various other authors, Shirley has published seven novels and number of poetry books. She has written numerous short stories. Her latest fiction is *Sparks in the Wind* soon to be released electronically. Shirley's written Eclipse Court at www.eclipsecourt.blogspot.com and is currently writing Kyrus Talain at www.kyrustalain.blogspot.com.

She's swung a sword on a movie set, studied karate, and shiatsu, taught women, children and the differently-abled self-defense, rolled off the back of a horse more than once, and found out how much fun hang-gliding is. Her eyes are brown, her hair… currently… is tortoiseshell.

Bettina Meister: Bettina Meister, 40-something for the next years, lives in the countryside of Northern Hessia. Although currently a social education worker, her desire is to be a fulltime author. Her love for writing covers Steampunk in particular as well as historical subjects in general, including cooking (her first book is on cooking on the emigration ships of the 18th to 20th century). Apart from writing, she shares the lives of her two cats and her distinctive other, loves reading, genealogy, and is editor of an online-magazine on fiction: www.zauberspiegel-online.de

Chris Morris: Author and composer Chris Morris began writing music in 1966, fiction in 1984, and nonfiction in 1989, as a Senior Fellow and Research Director at the U.S. Global Strategy Council in Washington, D.C. His musical credits include the album "The Christopher Morris Band" (MCA) and "Everybody Knows" (Singing Horse). Much of his fiction and nonfiction literary work, including all his book-length science fiction and fantasy, has been written in collaboration with his wife, Janet Morris. Chris Morris's nonfiction work includes *Nonlethality: A Global Strategy, The Age of Chaos: Nonlethality, Information Warfare, and Airpower,* and the book, *The American Warrior.* Chris Morris's novels, co-written with Janet Morris, include the Threshold series, *The 40-Minute War*, *Outpassage*, and three Sacred Band of Stepsons novels, *City at the Edge of Time*, *Tempus Unbound*, and *Storm Seed*, as well as the full-length *Heroes in Hell* novel, *The Little Helliad.* He has contributed short fiction to the best-selling series *Thieves' World* and *Heroes in Hell* and written on a range of national security topics.

Janet Morris: Best-selling author Janet Morris began writing in 1976 and has since published more than 20 novels, many co-authored with her husband Chris Morris or others. She has contributed short fiction to the shared universe fantasy series Thieves' World, in which she created the Sacred Band of Stepsons, a mythical ancient cavalry unit modeled on the Sacred Band of Thebes. She created, orchestrated, and edited the Bangsian fantasy series *Heroes in Hell*, writing stories for the series as well as co-writing the related novel, *The Little Helliad*, with Chris Morris. Most of her fiction work has been in the fantasy and science fiction genres, although she has also written historical and other novels. Janet Morris has written, contributed to, or edited several book-length works of non-fiction, as well as papers and articles on nonlethal weapons, developmental military technology and other defense and national security topics.

Robert M. Price: Robert, a fan of H.P. Lovecraft since the Lancer paperback collections of 1967 appeared, began writing scholarly articles and humorous pieces on HPL and the Cthulhu Mythos in 1981. His celebrated semi-pro zine, *Crypt of Cthulhu,* began as a quarterly fanzine for the Esoteric Order of Dagon Amateur Press Association in 1981 and made it to 109 issues. In 1990 he began editing Mythos anthologies for Fedogan & Bremer and Chaosium, Inc. and still does! His fiction has been collected in *Blasphemies and Revelations.* Centipede Books will soon be issuing his five-volume annotated edition of the fiction of H.P. Lovecraft.

Bill Snider: AKA: Zombie Zak – Created in Toronto, Canada by mad scientists of psychotic intent, is the author of *Chaptered and Versed, Poetic and Cursed,* a collection of dark and zombirific poetry. With a story in *Rogues in Hell* and a pot full of poems in the anthology *Old School*, he has plans for global domination, in which you may join or refrain (your choice, really!). The Apocalypse has already begun; you just don't know it yet. But ZZ does and is loving it! Vive la Dead! Feed him, fear him, but don't leave your cookies near him.

Come visit him at: ZombieZak.com or on Facebook and Twitter and all that stuff.

ABOUT THE EDITORS

John Manning, Editor-in-Chief: Known widely throughout North Texas for his expertise at arranging gaming programs for fan conventions, and as a Regional Director for TSR's Role Play Games Association. *What Scares the Boogey Man?* is John's first foray into the world of professional editing. A communications major in college, his studies included literature and grammar, as well as radio, journalism (he was an editor for his college paper, *The Erie Square Gazette*), and drama. While stationed in Germany, he served as Press Liaison for *Stars and Stripes*, the U.S. Army's official publication. When not writing or editing, he also is a recruiter for an international travel company.

Meghan Graham, Associate Editor: Born and raised in North Texas, Meghan graduated from the University of North Texas in 2008. She has since spent three years as an administrator for PtME Productions tabletop RPGs, and been on staff for multiple gaming and anime conventions throughout Texas and Oklahoma since 2006. Currently, she spends her time as a recruiter for an international travel company, and as an associate editor for Fantom Enterprises. Her efforts have helped stories be accepted into the *Heroes and Hell* series by Janet and Chris Morris, the upcoming *Sha'Daa: Facets*, by Michael H. Hanson and Ed McKeown, and this collection from Fantom Enterprises, *What Scares the Boogey Man?*

Stormy Stogner-Medina, Associate Editor: Stormy has been writing and editing work since her teen years, long before she ever entered college. She lives in rural East Texas with her husband, three children, two cats, and her dog. She has an extensive background in Native American Studies, Women's Studies, and Literature. When she is not editing copy, she spends her time playing piano and designing and producing pieces in a variety of mediums including beads, fabric, and paint.

www.ingramcontent.com/pod-product-compliance
Lightning Source LLC
Chambersburg PA
CBHW030327030726

47499CB00003B/673